BRACED TO BITE

Berkley JAM titles by Serena Robar

BRACED TO BITE

FANGS FOR FREAKS

DATING FOR DEMONS

BRACED TO BITE

SERENA ROBAR

B
BERKLEY BOOKS, NEW YORK

THE BERKLEY PUBLISHING GROUP
Published by the Penguin Group
Penguin Group (USA) Inc.
375 Hudson Street, New York, New York 10014, USA
Penguin Group (Canada), 90 Eglinton Avenue East, Suite 700, Toronto, Ontario M4P 2Y3, Canada
(a division of Pearson Penguin Canada Inc.)
Penguin Books Ltd., 80 Strand, London WC2R 0RL, England
Penguin Group Ireland, 25 St. Stephen's Green, Dublin 2, Ireland (a division of Penguin Books Ltd.)
Penguin Group (Australia), 250 Camberwell Road, Camberwell, Victoria 3124, Australia
(a division of Pearson Australia Group Pty. Ltd.)
Penguin Books India Pvt. Ltd., 11 Community Centre, Panchsheel Park, New Delhi—110 017, India
Penguin Group (NZ), 67 Apollo Drive, Rosedale, North Shore 0632, New Zealand
(a division of Pearson New Zealand Ltd.)
Penguin Books (South Africa) (Pty.) Ltd., 24 Sturdee Avenue, Rosebank, Johannesburg 2196,
South Africa

Penguin Books Ltd., Registered Offices: 80 Strand, London WC2R 0RL, England

This is a work of fiction. Names, characters, places, and incidents either are the product of the author's imagination or are used fictitiously, and any resemblance to actual persons, living or dead, business establishments, events, or locales is entirely coincidental. The publisher does not have any control over and does not assume any responsibility for author or third-party websites or their content.

PRINTING HISTORY
Berkley JAM trade paperback edition / May 2006
Berkley trade paperback edition / June 2010

Berkley trade paperback ISBN: 978-0-425-23764-9

The Library of Congress has cataloged the Berkley JAM trade paperback edition as follows:

Robar, Serena.
    Braced 2 bite / Serena Robar.—Berkley trade paperback ed.
        p. cm.
    Summary: When Colby Blanchard is attacked and turned into a half-vampire, her senior year of high school becomes surreal as she vacillates between trying to save her life and worrying about losing her place on the cheerleading squad.
    ISBN 0-425-20976-8
    [1. Vampires—Fiction. 2. High schools—Fiction. 3. Schools—Fiction.] I. Title. II. Title:
Braced 2 bite.
    PZ7.R5312Br 2006
    [Fic]—dc22   2005035333

PRINTED IN THE UNITED STATES OF AMERICA

10 9 8 7 6 5 4 3 2 1

*For my mom who raised me to be
an independent, creative, kick-ass chick.
I love you.*

Acknowledgments

This book could not exist without the exhaustive efforts of one particular person . . . ME! But a few others made it possible as well, such as my personal patron of the arts, Jason Robar, who always believed in me (smart man), and my writing posse, Christina Arbini, Shannon Mc-Kelden Cave, Erin Eisenberg, Kelli Estes, Cara Kean and Barb Roberts. But mostly just ME!! Muahahahahaha . . .

One

woke up and stretched when my alarm went off at exactly 6:37 A.M. School would start at 7:45 and I needed forty-five minutes to get ready, seven minutes for breakfast and five minutes to get to school. Leaving me with eleven minutes before class started. Just enough time to casually flirt with Aidan Reynolds on my way to trigonometry.

I stood up and checked my appearance in the full-length mirror on the back of my bedroom door. I was checking for blotchy skin, or worse—*pimples*. After careful scrutiny I nodded in satisfaction. It was a game day and the last thing I needed was a huge zit on my chin.

"Today will be a great day. I, Colby Blanchard, will execute all of my dance routine perfectly. I will ace my trig exam and I will get Aidan to ask me to Homecoming."

I smiled at myself, confident that daily affirmation was the best way to start the day. I jumped into the shower and scrubbed every inch of my body. I took extra time to loofah my feet, knees and elbows. I liked them to be super-soft.

After drying off, I was carefully detangling my hair (why was I cursed with such super-fine hair?) when my mom knocked on the bathroom door.

"Honey, I have a showing this morning and your father has to leave early because of the visiting orthodontists. Remember, he's showing his new technique this morning so you have to take the bus to school today. Sorry."

What?! Now my schedule was totally screwed up.

"Mom! You should have told me last night. I didn't get up early enough to take the bus!"

"Guess you'll have to hurry."

I glared at the door that separated me from my mother. Would it have killed her to tell me last night? I sometimes wondered if I was switched at birth. The daughter of a real estate agent and an orthodontist was hardly the kind of stock I felt would mold me into all that I could be. I loved my parents, but I wanted much more out of life than selling homes and straightening teeth.

I decided to wear my long hair back in a French braid and tie it off with scrunchies in gold and purple to maximize my school spirit. Since it was a game day, I already had my cheerleading outfit ready. How could I shave another couple of minutes off of my morning?

I could hardly forgo makeup and I'd already modified my hairstyle, so the best I could do was take the back trail through the woods to school. It was much faster than taking the bus and really, how many sixteen-year-olds rode the bus? I would be the laughingstock of school if I did such a thing.

For the millionth time I crossed my fingers that my upcoming seventeenth birthday would result in a car, like I planned. I felt like the only licensed teenager on the Eastside who didn't have her own transportation.

Mom and Dad were already gone when I grabbed a bagel and swabbed it with fat-free cream cheese. I wanted to lose six pounds so I could stay on top of the pyramid. I'd overheard Allison talking about a weight check so she could take my place. That was so not gonna happen. I wasn't about to let her squeeze me out of my spot. I simply switched to diet soda and cut down on my meals. Sure, it was tough when everyone around me was munching chips and stuff, but I liked to be the smallest one on the squad, the one who got to be on top of the pyramids and do all the stunts.

I checked my watch and slowed down a bit. I was five minutes ahead of schedule. Sitting down at the kitchen table, I munched quietly, thinking about the day ahead and making a mental list of things to do:

—Update BlackBerry to include weekend plans
—Make final list of invitees to my seventeenth b-day party

—Get streamers and supplies from Mrs. Frost to decorate
varsity football team's lockers
—Check reference book in library on World War II, Battle
of the Bulge, for history class

I looked around the table for my BlackBerry, deciding it
was easier to input this stuff than try to commit it to memory,
when the headline of the *Seattle PI* caught my attention.

EASTSIDE ATTACKER STILL AT LARGE

Great, this stupid "attacker" was still out there scaring
parents half to death and keeping game attendance to a mini-
mum. I didn't understand the big deal. Here was some loser
who liked to follow teenage girls and scare them. He hadn't
hurt any of them—well, except for the last girl a week ago.
But he only pushed her down. How incompetent were the police that they couldn't catch this guy?

I checked my watch again and decided it was time to go. I
slipped on my letterman jacket (second year of varsity cheer
squad, thank you very much) and slung my backpack over
one shoulder. It was mid-October in the Pacific Northwest,
which meant the mornings and evenings were cool but the
days were still warm. I headed out the door.

I walked toward the bus stop but veered right onto a trail
that was blocked off by cement posts. This was the back
route to school, through a wooded area alongside a ravine
that featured a seasonal creek.

Just ahead of me I noticed my neighbor, Piper Prescott. Piper and I were best friends in elementary school but we drifted apart in junior high when she discovered black eyeliner and somber clothing, and now we just exchanged nods in the hallway. Odd thing about growing up. Location creates best friends and then fashion, culture and cliques divide them again.

Piper glanced behind her and slowed down when I waved. We might not hang out in high school but we could walk together in the woods. Anyone could walk together in the shadow of trees. It was in the bright glaring sunlight that cliques stayed with their own.

"It's a game day. Where is your school spirit?" I asked, reviewing her black hooded sweatshirt, torn jeans and black combat boots.

"I am loaded with team spirit." She smirked and pulled her hoodie up to reveal a very faded T-shirt emblazed with our school mascot, the Eagle.

"I stand corrected. For a minute there I was afraid you had an eagle tattooed on your stomach." Which wasn't such a far-off thought considering Piper had a row of piercings in her ears and one in her nose. She may even have had her tongue pierced, but I couldn't be sure.

"Tattoo the memory of this lame school on my skin forever? Hah!"

"What's wrong with our school?"

"It creates a bunch of zombies that just go with the flow and don't have an original thought in their heads."

It was an ancient difference of opinion that stemmed from the beginning of the end of our hanging out together. That and the fact that I didn't own anything black.

"Ah yes, you're battling 'The Man,' " I retorted. "I keep forgetting how oppressed you are, what with living in the poor part of town and all."

This was a sore point with Piper. Her parents were loaded with cash earned during the booming computer era. They were die-hard Republicans and she lived in the nicest house on the golf course.

"Humph." Piper snorted and kicked the fallen leaves as we walked. It was tough to debate the facts when I had eaten so many snacks in her kitchen overlooking the greens of the fourth hole.

"So, pretty weird about all those attacks, huh?" I asked after a moment of silence.

"I'm not supposed to be walking to school anymore."

"Yeah, me neither." I was pretty sure that was what my mother was implying when she left the newspaper on the table.

We continued to walk, side by side.

"Aren't you a little worried?" I ventured.

"Me? No way. You should be, though. All those other girls were Barbie dolls, just like you."

I nodded at her. "Nice one. Didn't even see that coming."

"I try. Seriously though, the last three girls to be harassed all had long blonde hair."

"Yeah, but they weren't seriously hurt, though. Someone was just messing with them." I tried to sound confident.

Piper rolled her eyes at me in that superior way of hers that bugged the crap out of me.

"You are so clueless," she said and kicked a rock out of the way.

"I'm sure that summer in Europe with your parents last year has matured you more than any of us at this lame school," I snapped back icily. Maybe walking with Piper was a mistake. I picked up the pace to pass her.

"He's building up his courage," Piper murmured softly.

I slowed down and looked at her. "What?"

She cleared her throat and replied, "He is building up his courage. First he just scares them but then he'll get bored with that and take it to the next level."

"Like pushing someone down?" I asked, thinking of the last girl attacked.

She nodded. "Exactly."

"So now you're an expert on attackers?" I said derisively, maybe because it frightened me that she was actually making sense.

"It's what they all do." She stopped, pulled her backpack off and opened it. I peeked inside and saw a stack of books. On the top was one about serial killers.

"A little light reading before going to bed?" I asked her, eyes wide with surprise.

She zipped the pack shut and swung it back on.

"I like to be informed." Her eyebrow arched delicately as she said it, as though to imply, "Unlike you."

We started walking again.

"Hey, I'm all for education but isn't that a little morbid thinking? After all, no one has been seriously hurt."

"Yet," she pointed out.

We walked a couple of more paces while I absorbed that bit of information.

"When did you get so dark?" The question I was thinking popped out before I knew what I said.

"When did you get so stupid?" She looked at me meaningfully.

"I'm a 4.0 student, taking all advanced placement classes, Piper. I am far from stupid." I glared at her, more offended that she thought I was stupid than ignorant.

"You *are* book smart. But you're completely clueless about life."

She said this with such a patronizing tone, as though she had seen all the world had to offer and could get by just fine, but *I* would be gang fodder on the streets in mere minutes.

"Thank you kindly for your psychoanalysis. Next time I need the opinion of a Goth burnout, you'll be the first one I call." It was unfair and childish of me, but she made me so mad sometimes.

She just smirked at me and I resisted the urge to kick her. Exchanging barbs with Piper was like sneaking up on a porcupine. It was kind of interesting until you got stabbed.

The back of the school yard came into view and she surprised me by saying, "Seriously, you should be more careful."

I answered her in my most snarky voice. "I'll take it under advisement."

She muttered, "Whatever," and crossed the trail to the school. We both knew I wasn't going to stop walking to school via the backwoods. Nor was I going to run to our library and check out the Green River Killer's biography. I firmly believed I was no more likely to get attacked walking to school than any other person. Blonde hair be damned. This morning I walked with Piper. There was safety in numbers. And besides, there was no way I would risk my reputation by arriving on school grounds emerging from a big yellow bus. Nada. None.

Once I was sure Piper was far enough away from me, I turned toward the school as well. The length of a football field separated us. I would arrive at school through the back door and she would arrive using the side entrance. No one would know we spoke and I was fine with that. Not that I considered myself too good for Piper. At least she wasn't like that awful Rebecca Conway, the self-appointed leader of the Goths.

Rebecca, who currently referred to herself as Diva Raine, was my arch nemesis. Raine had inky black hair, white skin and probably bought more black eyeliner and lipstick than anyone in the Eastside. Walgreen's had to give her a frequent buyer discount.

I shared advanced creative writing with her and every assignment was the same thing from her: death. Death is beautiful, death is release, death is another state of the living, blah, blah, blah. IMHO, if she liked death so much she should do us all a favor and take it to the next level so we wouldn't have to hear her jabber about it anymore.

I reached my locker by the first bell and glanced around for Aidan. Lots of students were jostling about, laughing and getting ready to start their day, but no Aidan. I checked my reflection in the locker mirror and decided to touch up my lip gloss. Just then Raine walked by with her lemmings and purposely bumped into me, hoping to smear my gloss. Luckily, I was able to avert disaster.

"Oops, Diva Raine didn't mean to bump you, Cheesy." I couldn't figure out what was more annoying. The fact that she had nicknamed me Cheesy (which was hardly a far stretch since my name was Colby, after all) or that she referred to herself in the third person. The chick was weird. Out-and-out weird.

"No problem, *Rebecca*," I said, stressing her full name. "I can't imagine you see very well with all that black eyeliner. Reminds me of our football team."

I brightened with dramatic delight. "Why, what a wonderful way of showing your school spirit on game day, *Rebecca*."

I applauded her with a huge grin on my face. Others watching the exchange began applauding too. Pretty soon Raine's face was no longer white, but red from outrage. She hissed at me and stormed off amid the laughter.

I don't know what she was thinking, trying to one-up me on my own turf. Was she truly that delusional? I took one last glance around for Aidan, then at my locker clock. There would be no opportunity for flirting this morning. I would update my BlackBerry to fit it in at lunch. If I didn't get to it, how could I expect Aidan to ask to drive me home after the game tonight? Or better yet, take me to an after-game party?

I grabbed my trig book and notebook before shutting the locker door to go to class. I passed Raine by her locker and pretended I didn't see her. Her eyes practically bore holes in my back. If looks could kill, I would have been a goner. But then, if that were true, I would have died a thousand times by now. It may seem cool to wax poetic about eternal sleeping and the undead but it took real courage to embrace life and actively seek out success. What was life if one didn't live it fully? Seemed like a big waste to me.

I sat down in trig next to my best friends Marci and Rachel. Both were cheerleaders and both took AP classes too. Marci was a brunette with soft curls and Rachel wore her auburn hair short and chic. We made a pretty impressive sight when we were shopping at the mall or cheering. In fact, no matter where we went, we attracted a lot of attention.

"Where were you last night?" Marci asked me as I sat down. "I didn't get your homework e-mail until really late. Look at these dark circles." She gestured to her sparkling brown eyes and flawless skin. She looked fine to me, so I shrugged.

"I did the homework last night. It was just a little tougher than I planned." It took me an extra hour to do, which really messed with my study schedule.

"Fine, at least I got it," she grumbled and I had to stamp down a little annoyance. I was flattered at first when Marci asked me to tutor her, but when we got together we would end up going shopping or rearranging each other's closets. It was easier just to let her review my homework so she could see the work on any problems she didn't understand. But now I think she was blatantly copying all my homework and not even trying to do it on her own.

Rachel was asking my opinion on her new eye shadow when Aidan walked into class. Everything else sort of melted away and all I could see were his broad shoulders and high-lighted hair. His eyes were so blue, where mine were closer to gray. We would make such a perfect Homecoming King and Queen.

I turned away from Rachel to smile at him as he walked by.

He nodded to me with a half smile. " 'Sup?"

He passed by and slid into his seat at the back of the class.

My classes went by in a blur, and I finally came across Aidan at the end of lunch. I was sure my smile was brilliant and food-free since I wasn't eating much and I always brushed my teeth after lunch, no matter how little I ate. It kept my breath fresh and my smile sparkling.

When you live with an orthodontist, the first thing you learn to do is keep your smile in great shape. My father tended to stare at my teeth when I was talking. I learned when

I was twelve and first started wearing braces that Dad's intense focus when I talked had nothing to do with what I was saying and everything to do with analyzing how quickly my teeth were being corrected.

If I had to quote advice from my father to take into the "real" world it would have to be, "Don't forget to floss." Yeah, flossing is big with my dad.

"Hey, Aidan." I smiled as I leaned against my locker.

"Hey." He nodded toward me and I almost sighed when he raked his hand through his blond hair to keep it out of his clear blue eyes. We'd hooked up at several parties and now it was time to make our "relationship" more official. At least, that was my plan.

"Big game tonight. You guys ready for it?"

Okay, so I sounded kind of dorky. I wasn't used to small talk. I'm a person who likes to get to the point right away but high school is not like that. There are rules.

"Yeah! Those Bulldogs are goin' home with their tails between their legs. We're gonna kick ass!" His fellow players, who usually surrounded him, whooped and hollered while chest-slamming each other in excitement. A chorus of "Go Eagles" echoed down the hall.

"Go Eagles!" I reciprocated to the mob and turned my attention back to Aidan.

"So, what's the 411 on after-game festivities?" I tried to sound nonchalant. A guy didn't like to be chased. He needed to pursue me, but I could nudge him in the right direction.

"Depends on if we win or lose. How about we hook up after the game and go from there?"

I nodded thoughtfully, but inside my stomach was doing flip-flops. "It could work. Let's play it by ear."

"That's cool," he responded. In teen talk, we had just made our first unofficial date. Things were progressing right on schedule.

* * *

We won the game and spirits were high. Afterward, I waited outside for Aidan to make his appearance. Other players kept streaming out of the locker room. I finally lost my patience and told Brad McGraw, our star receiver, to let Aidan know I was waiting for him. Brad looked confused when he said, "Aidan's not in there, Colby. He left a half hour ago with Allison."

I tried not to scream "What?!" in poor Brad's face. Instead I nodded weakly as Brad shrugged and left me alone.

I don't know how long I stood outside with my mouth hanging open like a complete fool, but I imagine it was a while. When I finally pulled myself together I noticed I was the only one left from my cheer squad. Marci and Rachel were nowhere to be seen. They must have headed off when I assured them that Aidan was giving me a ride home. Now what was I going to do?

Mom and Dad were already home, having left at the beginning of the fourth quarter since our team was so far ahead. I assured them I was getting a ride with Aidan as well.

I wondered who I *hadn't* told I was riding back with Aidan. My humiliation on Monday would be huge if I didn't do some damage control this weekend. Maybe I could save face at DeLynn's party tomorrow?

I should have been clearer when Aidan and I had talked earlier today. He probably took my "let's play it by ear" to mean "not interested," and before I knew it, Allison had usurped my position and wheedled her way into Aidan's evening plans and his car. Now I would have to walk home.

I tightened my backpack over the bulk of my letterman jacket and headed in the direction of my house. I would use the trail behind the school that Piper and I had used this morning. It meant walking alone in the evening without any lampposts, but the football stadium lights were still on and I was hoping they would stay that way for the next fifteen minutes. It was only a quarter of a mile through the woods so I should be fine.

I was grateful that it wasn't too cool that evening. However, the dew was already playing havoc with my cheer shoes, not to mention the difficulty I was having walking at a brisk pace with a backpack over a letterman jacket. The smell of wet leaves and sound of the seasonal creek was my only company. I could feel the sweat seep into the acrylic fibers of my cheer sweater. It would definitely need a trip to the ol' dry cleaner before our next game. I didn't even want to think about the BO issue.

It was these thoughts—sweaty sweaters and stinky armpits—that kept me distracted enough not to hear the sound of footsteps in the leaves. When I realized someone else was on the path, they were literally right behind me. Big dope that I am, I was busier thinking about my clothes than my surroundings.

I picked up the pace and adjusted my backpack, nonchalantly peeking over my shoulder to catch a glance behind me. I was surprised to see absolutely no one. The stadium lights still glowed so the path was fairly well lit. I breathed a sigh of relief. *Guess it was a rabbit or something.* I decided to take off my jacket and tie it around my waist for the rest of the trip home. It would keep my legs a little warmer. I was just starting to put my pack back on when the stadium lights went out, leaving me in total darkness.

"Crap," I muttered, waiting for my eyes to adjust to the evening. There was still a moon out, so I could see down the trail, but without the glowing overhead lights, I was feeling a lot more vulnerable.

"Colby." I thought I heard my name whispered when a slight breeze stirred up the leaves.

"Piper?" I whispered tentatively.

Silence. I waited another moment. I must have imagined it and took another couple of steps.

"Don't leave." The soft voice rasped again.

I spun around and nobody was there.

At this point, in all major horror movies, the stupid, solitary cheerleader (that part to be played by *moi*) would run away from the voice and trip over some lame obstacle so the killer/monster could attack her easily. Not being a fan of the genre, I stood my ground and said, "Okay, enough screwing around. Come out."

It wasn't bravery or bravado that compelled me to confront this unseen tormentor. It was really the immortality of youth. I didn't believe for one minute that the Eastside Attacker happened to be on the same trail in the backwoods as I was on a Friday evening. The odds were extremely unlikely. Also, those types of things didn't happen to me. I was the one who won first place in debate and trophies for cheer squad. I was not attacked by some loser in the dead of night. That happened to other people. Not to me.

So imagine my surprise when a familiar-looking guy stepped out of the darkness to stand in front of me. I should have been afraid. I should have screamed and run and did all that stuff, but oddly enough, I wasn't scared. After all, this was just a kid, hardly older than I was, nondescript with soft brown hair and eyes, wearing jeans and a sweater. It was like walking down the mall and running into every guy I ever met rolled into one. I was sure I had seen him at the football game.

"Are you trying to give me a heart attack?"

He looked mildly surprised and shook his head no.

"What are you doing here?" I asked him, still irritated.

"Following you," he said simply, still keeping his distance.

"Why?" I demanded, now starting to feel a prick of unease.

"Because you're walking alone in the dark and it's not safe," he replied.

I let out a whoosh of air, surprised I was holding my breath. I couldn't think of his name, but he did have a face that I was certain I knew. Maybe he went to my school. A lot of people knew who I was because of cheer squad so it wasn't unusual that I wouldn't know his name.

"Oh, that's nice of you but I'm okay really," I assured him as I walked past him.

"I've heard a lot about you," he said softly, matching my pace.

Great, I have a new admirer.

"Really? That's nice," I said, mentally trying to figure out how close I was to the main street.

"No, not nice stuff at all."

And this was the point I started to get the creepy chills up my back and neck.

Two

I laughed nervously. "Then you must be talking to the wrong people because I'm really very nice."

"Show me," he insisted and suddenly I found myself face-to-face with him.

People react differently when cornered. Some freeze, others panic and some keep their cool. I fall under a different category. I get mad.

"Look, I'll show how nice I am by not kneeing you in the groin. Get out of my way!"

He looked me deep in the eyes and reached forward to sweep some hair away from my face. I stood frozen in place. I just couldn't get my feet to cooperate with my mind and run.

"You're very pretty," he whispered, moving closer to me until I could see how large his pupils were in the dim light.

"And you're very creepy," I replied, glad my voice still worked even if my body wasn't cooperating.

He stared at me intently and my body seemed to go numb. He leaned forward to kiss me and I surprised us both by saying, very firmly, "No."

He was startled. I could tell by the way he stopped and looked at me again.

"No," I said again, this time with more strength, and the feeling returned to my body.

"No!" I practically shouted and the cloudy spell that held my legs immobile seemed to give way. I pulled my knee up with as much force as I could muster and followed through with my threat. He was caught by surprise and grabbed at me as he buckled over. *Well, I did warn him.*

I struggled to pull away, but his hands were firmly gripping my sweater. He wrenched harder and I heard my sweater rip as I fell to my knees. I was free, for the moment. I tried to crawl away, but he yanked the backpack that was still draped across my arm and pulled me toward him.

He grabbed my shoulders and threw me back so I was faceup. I don't remember feeling fear, just anger. My sweater was ruined, I was rolling around on the dirty trail and I looked like a stupid turtle lying on its back, trying to turn over. Certainly not me at my best.

He grabbed my face and looked at me again. I rammed my head forward and hit him in the nose. I have seen this move in several action movies and can honestly say it hurts like hell. I didn't break his nose but I did startle him enough for his grip to weaken, allowing me to roll to my side and get to my knees. My stupid backpack was tangled around my arm, and as I struggled to get free I looked his way. He was also on his knees, holding his nose. I thought he might be bleeding.

He grabbed at my leg, and I tried to kick him away. He was very strong. I scratched at the dirt as he pulled me toward him.

He grabbed my hair and pulled my head back so I could see the trail clearly from my position on the ground. It was empty. He flipped me on my back again, this time fairly easily. I felt a sharp twinge in my neck where he was pulling my hair and my whole body went ramrod straight. My eyes were open, my mouth was open and I was stiff as a board.

I didn't feel anything. I couldn't move. I expected this would be the point where he would kill me, rape me, beat me—*something*. We seemed to be in that position for an eternity when he shifted.

He put his arm to my mouth and forced it open wider. I felt a warm liquid enter my mouth and I gagged. He was poisoning or drugging me! My strength returned and I screamed, "No!" a final time, pushing him with all my might, punching him in the nose again. We both struggled to our feet. I was ready to run but he grabbed me by the throat and held me up. For someone who looked so average, he was amazingly strong.

My feet were dangling in the air and I was clutching at his hands. He was having a tough time keeping a good grip on me because I struggled so. He finally lost his temper. I went sailing through the air like a rag doll. I remember hitting a tree, hearing a sickening crunch and rolling down the ravine. Then I couldn't remember anything.

*   *   *

I must have been dreaming about sleeping in my warm bed, snuggled deep into the down comforter, because the realization that I was actually facedown, partially submerged in a creek was somewhat of a shock, to say the least. The ravine was neither warm nor snuggly.

I looked up at the sky, noting it was dark, and wondered how long I had been out. Five minutes, an hour? It was tough to tell. Rarely did I wear a watch and my cell phone was in my backpack, which I had lost in the struggle. I held out little hope that the attacker had kindly left me the bag or my warm letterman jacket. It was time to drag myself out of the little stream and look around. It took awhile as I was pretty far down the hillside, practically entombed under a large bush.

Wiping my brow from the effort of crawling upward, I realized I was covered in mud and my cheek stung. I rubbed it and winced. Sure enough, it was scraped, as were my knees and my shoulder. I was achy but surprisingly spry considering some fruitcake had just thrown me down a hill.

Looking around in case my attacker decided to reappear, I slowly made my way up the side of the ravine. I'm sure I looked ridiculous crawling two paces, then freezing to listen if anyone was around, but hey, I didn't need another run-in with the East-side Attacker. All I wanted to do was get home. Home was safe.

When I made it to the top, I took a cursory look around for my jacket and bag without any luck. Like I thought, good as gone. I hurried home and was surprised how quickly I managed it. Very little traffic out confirmed my fear that it was much later than I had originally thought. If it was past my curfew, I would be grounded for sure. My parents were pretty strict about that and I had no intention of telling them I'd been attacked. I didn't feel like adding an hour of "I told you so's" and a trip to the police department to my already ruined evening.

Considering the attack, I was thrilled to arrive home without anyone following me. I was sure he was ready to strike again and finish the job. I couldn't relax until I was safely inside.

Then I would have to make up a whopper of a tale why I was late getting home. How was I going to explain the way I looked? I just wanted to forget the whole thing. Take a nice hot bath and let the steamy water cleanse the experience away.

I walked through the back door, into the kitchen where my mother appeared to be preparing dinner. This would be odd if my mom wasn't famous for cooking when she worried. Guess I was later than I thought.

I walked up behind her and said, "Hey."

I startled her, causing the dicing knife in her hand to slip and slash her palm, deeply.

"God, Mom, I'm sorry. Let me help."

She stood frozen, looking at the cut then staring at me with an incomprehensible expression on her face. I imagined it was the look I must wear whenever Aidan talked to me. One of shock, relief and denial, all in one. Not the most attractive look. I would have to work on that one.

I grabbed my mom's wrist to move her toward the sink when the scent of her flowing blood filled my nostrils. My throat constricted in thirst, I felt a flash of pain in my jaw and before I knew what I was doing, I put my mouth to her cut to stop the bleeding.

At least I thought I was going to stop the bleeding. Instead, I kind of sucked the blood. I was so thirsty and it felt like the most refreshing water after running a long race in the hot sun. The cut was deep, so I didn't have to suck hard, just open my throat and let the blood pour in. In a very short time I licked the cut and it immediately stopped. I pulled away to look at it and was surprised to see the cut was practically healed. It was as though a week had passed since she hurt herself.

I looked up at my mom in horror when the reality of what I'd just done sunk in. She wore a dazed look on her face. Her eyes were unfocused and her lips formed a small 0 of surprise. She didn't seem to be in pain. She seemed to be in shock.

"Mom?" I asked uncertainly and then her eyes came into focus, staring at me. Then she screamed at the top of her lungs. I jumped back, putting my hands over my ears as my dad rushed into the room with Great-Aunt Chloe hot on his heels.

Dad caught sight of me first and he let out a very nonmasculine shriek himself. He positioned himself between Mom and me in a protective gesture.

The only one who seemed to keep her cool was Great-Aunt Chloe, which wasn't surprising since she was deaf as a post without her hearing aid and could barely see five feet in front of her due to cataracts. Actually she was my great-great-aunt but I always shortened it to great-aunt or aunt so she didn't feel so old.

"What's all this caterwauling about? Goodness gracious . . ." She took a moment to recognize me and threw open her arms in welcome.

It is surprising that the one person who would greet me with such unreserved joy was the one relative I rarely saw. But she at least seemed happy to see me so I rushed into her arms and hugged her back. She smelled like rose water and vanilla wafers. I never noticed that before. I used to think she smelled like old person, but not tonight. Tonight she smelled wonderful.

"Oh child! We thought you were done for. Our prayers have been answered," she crooned, hugging me even tighter. For a frail old woman of eighty something, she had quite a grip to her.

"Exactly how late for curfew am I?" I asked tentatively, surprised by her relieved declarations.

My aunt gave a dry cackle of relief. "Why, dear, you've been gone since Friday night—nearly forty-eight hours. We've had the police scouring the neighborhood for you. There is a candlelight vigil at your school right now."

"Really?" I asked, surprised. Could I have been unconscious in that ravine for nearly two days?

"Let me look at you." Aunt Chloe pulled away and held my face in her hands. Since she was barely five foot, I had to bend over quite a bit to give her a good look.

"Hmmm," she said as she peered into my face. "What color are your eyes, dear?" she asked me.

"Uh, blue," I responded.

She raised an eyebrow at me.

"Okay, fine. They're gray. Sometimes I wear colored contacts to make them look bluer." *Sheesh*.

"When was the last time you saw some sun?"

"What do you mean?" Sure, we lived in the Pacific Northwest and it rained quite a bit, but I was usually a lovely golden shade thanks to the advances in tanning-booth technology. "I tanned just yesterday so I would look good cheering at the game. Why?"

"You're white as a ghost, my dear. And your eyes are a funny shade."

"What kind of funny shade?" I pulled away, looking for something shiny. My father was surprisingly helpful as he was holding a heavy copper teakettle in his hand. I tried to ignore the menacing way he yielded it when I took it from him and looked at myself in the surface of the kettle. My eyes did look different, lighter. The copper was skewing the color but they definitely didn't look gray, or blue for that matter.

"I need a better mirror." I walked past my aunt into the family room and ducked into the small bathroom there. I took one look at myself and screamed.

They all came running at the sound of my distress. My parents might have been leery of me in the kitchen, but the sound of their only child screaming kicked the primal protection gene in gear.

My hair was a matted, muddy mess. No surprise considering I'd been sleeping with the mushrooms and blackberry brambles for the last two nights, but it was my skin and eye color that held me transfixed. My skin was pale. Not pale as in, "I haven't been to the Tannery in a while," but pale as in, "I've never seen the light of day before." It was almost translucent, obvious despite the dirt and scrapes on my face. If I didn't know better, I would have sworn I was very ill . . . or a Goth.

Then there were my eyes. My very yellow eyes. Gone was the gray of years past. Now they were a glowing yellow. Ugh.

"What—what happened to me?" I stuttered. Could this be a common side effect of getting terrorized, like someone's hair turning white overnight?

"Where have you been? What happened to you?" My mother finally spoke for the first time, rubbing her palm with her other hand. She didn't say a word about my drinking her blood, for which I was thankful; but still, add that to the yellow eyes and white skin and I would have been running for the hills if I were her. Amazing woman, my mom.

"Well, after the game I walked home." No need to get into the humiliating details of how Aidan took out Allison instead of me.

"I took the, uh, back route." I looked up at them expecting to be chastised about walking through the woods at night with an attacker at large in the neighborhood, but they were silent.

"I was almost to the road when some guy stepped out of the shadows and he, he, threw me down." My mother gasped and reached out to hug me but my father put his arm out to stop her.

"Go on," he said.

"Well, I kneed him and fought but he held me down easily. He pinched my neck and I sort of froze in shock. I kept fighting him and that made him really mad.

"He picked me up and threw me into the ravine. I woke up and came straight home. I had no idea I was unconscious for two days."

I was really embarrassed about what happened to me. Maybe it was wrong to purposely leave out that the Attacker made me drink something. I didn't feel like having my stomach pumped and besides, if it was poison I would have been dead by now. It must have been something to make me sleep, since two days had passed.

I pushed my way out of the bathroom past them, where they stood frozen in the doorway, and sat down on the burgundy couch in our family room. I grabbed one of the chenille pillows and hugged it to my chest. This small gesture of normalcy made me feel better. Whenever I was feeling bad, I would cuddle up with a pillow on the couch and try to sort things out.

They followed me slowly.

"Is that all that happened?" Dad asked me softly, almost afraid of my answer.

"Yes, Dad. That is all that happened. Isn't it enough?" I asked angrily. I was pissed at myself but it seemed easier to yell at him. Dad had broad shoulders; in my state of mind, he could handle this burden better than I could right now.

"Honey, we need to get you to a doctor and get you checked out," my father said to the group.

"No!" The women shouted at once, surprising him and each other.

It was Aunt Chloe who offered the short-term solution. "I will give her a checkup. I didn't spend fifty-plus years as a nurse and survive two wars that I can't manage a common physical."

Aunt Chloe stood up and gestured for me to follow her to the spare bedroom. Apparently she had heard of my disappearance and had moved in from the local retirement village to help my family through this tough time.

"Marilyn, could you please join me? John, you stay here and for goodness sake, don't call anyone or do anything until we are done."

Dad nodded as he sank down in his favorite recliner, dropping his head into his hands.

I obediently followed Aunt Chloe and Mom into the spare bedroom and sat down on the bed. Aunt Chloe searched through her bag and pulled out a few items. Blood pressure wrist band, stethoscope, thermometer, a large Baggie filled to the rim with pill bottles that rattled around when she dropped it on the bed.

"Where did I put it?" she mumbled to herself and Mom and I shared a look. Mom patted my hand reassuringly and I smiled at her.

"Aha, here it is!" Aunt Chloe said triumphantly, brandishing a large magnifying glass in her hand. "Now, dear, let's get a good look at your neck. Where were you pinched?"

I was relieved she wanted to start there. I had no doubt if Dad was in charge, he would want to know if I had been molested in some way—and getting a pelvic exam by my great-great-aunt was not my idea of a good time.

I pulled my hair to the side and showed her the spot.

"Marilyn, could you get me a warm washcloth so we can clean up her neck a little bit?"

Mom jumped to do her bidding, anxious to be helping in any small way. When my neck was relatively dirt free, my aunt gazed at it through the looking glass and made a lot of *hmmm* and *ahh* sounds.

She pointed out a bruise to my mother where I was pinched and then identified two small incision marks, barely visible in the bruise.

My mother looked down at her hand, the one I'd sucked on, and showed it to my great-aunt, then proceeded to tell her what I did when I entered the kitchen. I squirmed in my seat, wishing I could run away and hide. I hear people do really odd things when they are in shock, but I doubted they nibbled on their mothers' hands and helped themselves to a blood cocktail.

Then Aunt Chloe wrapped a wide medical gadget on my wrist and turned it on.

"What's this?" I asked curiously, my wrist getting squeezed uncomfortably.

"It's my blood-pressure band. It helps me keep track of my high blood pressure—which is why I need those pills." She gestured to the overflowing Baggie.

I nodded and looked at the large digital face of the wrist band, which stayed suspiciously blank.

"Is it broken?" I asked when the LED registered only one pulse the entire time it was on my wrist.

"Don't think so. Marilyn, let's do you." She took the cuff off of me and put it on my mom.

Mom's reading showed an unusually high blood pressure, which was understandable considering the situation, and a decent pulse rate.

They both looked at the cuff, then me, pursing their lips in speculation. At that moment, I saw the family resemblance perfectly.

"Let's take her temperature," Mom suggested as she picked up an ancient-looking thermometer. She took it into the bathroom to wash. She walked back shaking the mercury down and put it under my tongue.

I sat obediently, the glass stick placed awkwardly under my tongue. After a minute, they read the thermometer and then stared at me strangely.

"Ninety-eight point six?" I asked hopefully.

"Uh, no," my mom replied, less than helpfully.

Aunt Chloe took her stethoscope out and listened to my heart and lungs. She nodded in satisfaction, putting her tools of the trade back in the bag. She took her time tidily arranging all of her things. Mom sat down next to me again and held my hand. When Aunt Chloe was done straightening things up, she stood up and made her medical pronouncement.

"Well, technically you're dead," she announced with flourish.

Three

"But you're obviously not dead, or you wouldn't be walking around and talking. So you must be undead. My guess is a vampire."

"You've got to be kidding me!" I exclaimed incredulously. Surely ol' Aunt Chloe had lost it.

"Nope. Seen it before. In the war. We'd get those boys in with a toe tag but when we tried to move them they would sit up and grab the nearest person and have themselves a drink."

Mom and I gaped at her.

"Course, we couldn't have our dead lads feeding on our orderlies so we would have to, uh, make the toe tag official, so to speak."

"You mean you had to kill them? Again?"

"Stake through the heart. Wasn't an easy decision to make

but when you have so many men who are alive that need you and one who is beyond your help that could hurt them, well, the decision is obvious."

"Were there a lot of vampires?" I asked uneasily, still not sold on this hypothesis.

"No, I only came across three in my war days. Of course other units may have seen more. Some things we all understood but didn't talk about. I mean, back in the States, who would believe one of our soldiers had turned vampire?"

We both nodded our agreement. After all, it was far-fetched even to me, and I was supposed to be one.

"I thought vampires couldn't go out in the sunlight."

"They can't. Them toe-tagged boys arrived covered in a sheet, and we didn't just get wounded during office hours. It was war, Colby. People killing each other at all hours of the day and night."

My aunt looked so ferocious at that moment I could easily see a younger version, snapping out orders and operating on fallen soldiers. It didn't take much of a stretch to see this younger version breaking a chair leg and staking an undead vampire either. Her job was to protect the soldiers and she'd done it.

"But I was out all day, in the sunlight, while I was in the ravine. Okay, maybe not the sunlight 'cause it was cloudy but it was definitely daytime."

Aunt Chloe nodded thoughtfully.

"And fangs? What about fangs? I don't have any." I opened my mouth wide to prove my perfect smile was fang-free.

"What about feeding on your mother?" she countered.

I closed my mouth and looked down at my lap, ashamed. Good question. How was I going to defend that action?

My mom spoke up. "It's okay, honey. You didn't hurt me. If anything, you saved me from getting stitches. That cut was very deep and you healed it. I don't think you drank my blood at all. I'm not woozy—I feel fine."

I was grateful for her defense but couldn't let her minimize what I'd done.

"Mom, I may not have any fangs but I drank your blood. I just couldn't help myself. I smelled the blood and wanted it. I was just so thirsty. I didn't drink much," I assured her when I saw the look on her face. "As quick as the thirst came on, it went away. I was full pretty quick."

My mom stared at me in shock and horror. I'd never seen that look before—like she was afraid of me—and I couldn't bear it.

I dropped down to my knees in front of her and laid my head in her lap.

"Mommy, I'm sooo sorry. I promise I won't ever do it again. I won't hurt you, I promise. Please forgive me. Don't be scared of me." I sobbed into her lap, clutching her legs.

After a moment I felt her hands stroke my matted hair, like she did when I was a child begging for forgiveness. She crooned nonsense words to soothe me. I looked up at her and saw tears rolling silently down her cheeks. She braved a small smile and all I saw reflected in her eyes was love.

"There, now, that's better. See, being a vampire isn't the

end of the world. Course, things are gonna be a little different, but we can figure that out," Aunt Chloe reassured me.

"But I can't be a vampire, I don't have any fangs!" I protested again.

"Maybe they only come out when you are ready to feed?" she suggested.

"No, Colby didn't have any fangs when she was with me," Mom pointed out and I was grateful she didn't use the term "feed."

"Well, open your mouth. Let's take a look," Aunt Chloe commanded and I obeyed instantly.

She *ummm*ed a lot, counting my teeth and poking at them with her finger.

"You are missing some teeth," she declared after her inspection.

I looked at Mom helplessly.

"Yes, when she was twelve she had oral surgery and they removed six teeth. Her wisdom teeth, which hadn't broken through the gums yet, and two others."

Aunt Chloe squinted at my mother. "Those other two, were they canine teeth?"

Mom nodded. "Yes, then she had braces for a year and wore headgear at night."

"Well, that explains it then."

Mom and I looked at each other and her in confusion.

"What does?" I asked.

"Your fangs are gone, dear. Fangs are canine teeth. You had those removed. So your fangs can't grow now, can they?"

I opened my mouth but nothing came out when the logic of what she said sank in. It made sense. Before I drank my mom's blood, I'd experienced a throbbing pain in my mouth. More specifically, in my upper gums. Crap.

"Great! That's just great. Not only am I a vampire, but I'm a mutant vampire. I have no fangs."

"Well, I'd say the problem is a little more than that. How are you going to feed without fangs?"

"Feed?" I asked stupidly. "I'm not going to feed again, ever." I shivered at the thought of drinking more blood, but my stomach growled treacherously. My mind might revolt, but my body didn't seem to share the sentiment.

"Honey, your aunt is right. You are going to have to eat."

"No way. That is just gross."

"If you don't feed, you die," my aunt said matter-of-factly.

"Who says? I'm not like the other vampires. I can go out in sunlight. Maybe I can eat real food too." I stood up and walked to the door. "I'm going to make myself a tuna sand- wich right now." I marched out of the bedroom, straight past my father who seemed to be in the same position we'd left him in, and into the kitchen.

I opened the fridge and gasped when I saw how much food was stuffed inside. Casseroles, quiches, etcetera, filled the shelves. Mom must have been beside herself with worry.

I pushed the thought aside and pulled out the makings of a monster tuna sandwich.

By the time I was ready for my first bite, my aunt and mother joined me in the kitchen. Dad was suspiciously absent.

"Here it goes." I saluted them with my sandwich and took a bite. Not bad, but not as good as I remembered. A little on the bland side but it was sustenance nonetheless. I swallowed my first bite in triumph. Aha! I didn't need blood to survive. As long as I had sandwiches, I would be fine.

I was smiling smugly at the thought when my stomach revolted. I ran to the sink in time to throw up my victorious bite.

Aunt Chloe handed me a warm washcloth when I was done so I could wash my face (or wipe the smugness away). Regardless, I used it gratefully.

I rinsed out the sink then said flatly, "I am going to take a shower now." They let me skulk away without comment. After all, finding out you're a vampire was one thing, but adding I-told-you-so's was like getting kicked when you're down.

I turned on the shower and shed my uniform. It was ruined. I doubted it could be cleaned and then there was the tear in the sleeve of the sweater. Sighing, I looked at myself in the mirror to identify blonde hair, filthy and matted. I was surprised any of it had stayed tucked in its braid. The scrape on my cheek was encrusted with mud.

Disheartened, I examined my vampire hickey. It didn't seem fair that the first hickey I received would be from the unwanted affections of a psycho bloodsucker. Such is life. If only Aidan had given me a ride home Friday night, then maybe I would be looking at *his* hickey mark and I would still be a normal teenager.

When the mirror started to steam, I stepped into the shower and groaned in pleasure. I was so cold. It took a while, but the warm water invaded the coolness of my skin and I almost felt like myself. I washed my hair (gagging over the potent fragrance of essential herbs) and scrubbed my body. I was relieved and surprised to discover I didn't need to shave my legs or armpits. Maybe there was some advantage to being undead after all.

I jumped out of the shower and opened my favorite lotion. The overpowering scent of cinnamon pumpkin filled my senses. Ugh, maybe I would pass on the lotion. My super-sensitive sniffer was definitely not up to the new Fall Harvest Edition.

I moisturized my skin with an unscented drugstore brand, brushed out my hair and did all the normal things I did every day. This felt good. This was normal. When I was doing these things, *I* was normal.

After blow-drying my hair, I was delighted to find it fall perfectly into place past my shoulders. At least I was getting a good hair day out of this ordeal.

All of my foundation was too dark for my current, uh, shall we say *alabaster* complexion. I did try some blusher to give me a little lift but ended up wiping most of it off. When you're pale, less is more. I added a little pink gloss and skipped any eye makeup. I hardly wanted to call attention to my freakish yellow eyes.

I threw on some yoga pants and a tee that said "Cheer." It was time to face the family. Dad hadn't said a word, so I left it to Mom to fill him in on the details. As I walked out, I grabbed my sunglasses off the dresser and slipped them on.

I glanced at myself in the hallway mirror and thought, *Not bad*. If you knew me you would think I was a tad under the weather because of the pale skin, but other than that, I looked just like me. To my surprise, the bite and scratches had faded away in the shower. My skin looked perfect again.

It was close to 11 P.M. when I finally reemerged.

Dad was still nowhere to be seen but Mom was at the kitchen computer, surfing the Net, when I startled her.

"Argh!" she gasped, grabbing at her chest.

"Sorry. Didn't mean to scare you."

"I didn't even hear you walk up."

I looked down at my feet and wiggled one in her direction.

"No shoes," I told her.

"Obviously. So I have been doing a little research on the Web about your, uh, condition. Very interesting stuff."

I pulled up a chair next to her so I could see as well.

"What's this?" I pointed to a site by Demonic Angel with flickering candles and gargoyle gifs, black background and yellow fonts. The title of the page was simply "The Castle" and the red font of the letters appeared to be dripping down the page, as if they were made of blood.

"You've got to be kidding me," I said.

"Well, dear, to be honest, it's not like you can type vampires.com and get a nice text-friendly site filled with all the information you need to know about being one of the undead."

I hated to admit it, but Mom had a good point.

"Where's Aunt Chloe?" I asked, looking around the kitchen.

"In bed, poor dear. She was up with me all of last night and she only took a short nap today. I don't know what I would have done without her."

"What about Dad?"

"Your father needs a little time. I told him the situation and he headed into the office to work on a project. It helps him think."

That explained my father's not-so-surprising reaction to finding out his daughter was a vampire. Dad was all about avoiding unpleasantness. When things got tough, he took off to his office. He was an orthodontist for God's sake—what kind of work was he going to do on a Sunday night? Reorganize the teeth molds?

"Sure, I understand." I sighed. I understood all too well.

"We told the police you were found unharmed. They wanted to know if we were going to take you to the doctor and we told them it was taken care of and you had a clean bill of health. Just some minor bruises and a concussion from the fall."

"What did you tell them, exactly?"

I couldn't believe Mom would tell the truth, but she wouldn't want people to be lulled into a false sense of security by not reporting the attack either.

"I told them you were surprised by the attacker but fell down the ravine and hit your head, knocking you unconscious."

I nodded unhappily. It sounded better than the truth but either story made me look bad. I hated that.

"They want to question you, but I told them the doctor said you needed a couple of days to recover from your concussion. I figure that gives us enough time to make some plans."

Her comment startled me. "What kind of plans?"

"Well, first we research what we are up against and decide how we deal with your new, uh, identity. Then we make the appropriate changes so that you can lead as normal a life as possible."

My mom was so matter-of-fact. I was amazed by her calm demeanor. Not much fazed her—when she was faced with disaster, she was as cool as can be.

"That was an awful lot of 'we's,' Mom. *I'm* the vampire, you know."

"Yes, you are, but we are a family and what affects you, affects all of us. We stick together. That is what family does."

I couldn't help looking around the kitchen and giving her a look. "Yeah, but Dad is family and he's nowhere to be found."

She ignored both look and statement and pointed to something on the computer screen. "According to this, vampires must feed nightly or they go insane. They can't go out in sunlight or they burn up and die. They can be killed by a wooden stake to the heart or holy water thrown at their face. It doesn't say anything about a silver bullet. I thought vampires could be killed by a silver bullet."

"That would be werewolves, Mom."

"Really? Are you sure?"

I pointed to myself and said, "Hello? Vampire here. Silver bullets are for werewolves."

"Don't get sassy, young lady; it's not like you're an expert on vampires. You only just became one."

Truer words were never spoken.

"If vampires burn up in the sun, how come I slept in the ravine without dying? Also, how am I going to feed every night without fangs? Why can't I eat regular food?" I jumped up in agitation. They really should give you a manual or something when you turn undead.

"Excellent questions, but I think we need to do more research before we can sort out fact from fiction. By the way, Piper called when you were in the shower."

"Piper called? Why?" I asked, surprised.

"Maybe because she was worried about you. Really, Colby, is it so surprising people cared you disappeared?"

"Did Marci or Rachel call?"

"Well . . . no, but Rachel's mom did call yesterday to offer her assistance. I'm sure your friends were in shock and will stop by to see you tomorrow."

I thought about that for a moment, imagining Marci and Rachel's reaction to the news I was missing, possibly murdered. They were probably pretty shook up. But still, Piper was the one who had called to offer comfort to my mom—my two best friends hadn't even bothered.

"What did Piper say?"

"She was very relieved to hear you were okay. She helped rally the candlelight vigil at the school. She said it was a full house. She thought you would like that." Mom smiled at me.

Yep, the thought of a crowded auditorium full of mourning students holding candles and praying for my safe return did appeal to the drama queen in me.

"You know, she stopped by yesterday with a casserole from her mom. I almost didn't recognize her. Her hair is jet-black now, with burgundy underneath. She wears it in a flip." Mom *tsked*. "Such a free spirit. I wish she would lighten up on the black eyeliner. She has such pretty eyes."

Yes, on the eve of my rising from the dead, Mom was gossiping about Piper's current fashion and offering makeover advice. Life in the suburbs was pretty surreal at times.

Mom tried to stifle a yawn, so I put my hand on her shoulder.

"Mom, go to bed. I can do the research. I'll bookmark the sites that seem interesting. You look exhausted."

She patted my hand in reassurance and stood up. She looked me square in the face, pulling the sunglasses down my nose.

"I love you honey." There were tears in her eyes and she hugged me. Well, actually it felt closer to clutching me for dear life. As if she was afraid to let me go or I would disappear into thin air.

"I love you too, Mom." I patted her on the back and whispered, "It's okay Mom. I'm here, I'm safe. Everything's gonna be okay."

She pulled away, and wiped her eyes with the back of her hand.

"Of course it is. You're home now. I don't know what's come over me. Probably all that leftover emotion from you being missing and all. I'll head to bed. Are you tired?" she asked.

"Mom?" I said, pointing to myself. "Nightstalker, remember?"

She *tsked* her way upstairs and I was suddenly alone in the kitchen. Just me and the Demonic Angel hangin' in The Castle. After a couple hours of taking notes and surfing the Web I decided to head to my room to read a bit. Every site seemed to contradict the other about what a vampire was or wasn't. About what vampires could do or couldn't do. I figured I would start my own series of tests tomorrow to separate the fact from fiction.

Besides, I still had work to do for my World War II report and all this vampire minutiae was starting to depress me.

I grabbed two books and climbed up the stairs. Then I slipped into some pajamas, brushed my teeth and completed my nightly skin-care routine. I liked the normalcy of doing everyday things. I jumped into bed with my books.

About a half hour later I heard my dad opening the garage door and then enter the house. I knew he might stop by and see how I was doing so I took preventative measures.

"Hey, angel," he whispered from the doorway. I pretended to be asleep because I was still pretty pissed off he'd left so quickly, without even talking to me. Did he think I wanted to be some undead freak out of some form of teenage rebellion?

"I know you're awake, Colby." He sighed.

"How?" I asked, still turned away from him and curled in a ball.

"Because you always curl in a ball and face away from the door when you're pretending to sleep. When you're really asleep, you lie on your back and drool."

I huffed out my breath. I do NOT drool.

He walked into the room and sat on the bed. He gently stroked my back and leaned closer.

"I guess you're pretty angry with me right now."

I shrugged, but still didn't turn around.

"Sweetheart, don't hate me for what I did. Please."

I was surprised by his pleading tone. My father was always a confident, firm paternal figure, if not a little distant. The man begging me to still love him didn't sound like the man I knew at all.

"I don't hate you, Daddy. Okay, I'm mad at you but I don't hate you." *Sure, walking out on me when you discovered I was turned into a vampire hurt my feelings, but I don't think I would label it hate. Just extreme disappointment.*

"Honey, I can't go back in time and change what I did. I can only hope to make up for it now."

Okay, this conversation was just getting weird. So he hid in his office until he could get a grip, it wasn't like he tried to stake me or something.

"Dad, are we talking about the same thing here?"

"I'm not sure, what do you think we're talking about?"

"Duh, the way you ran out of the house and completely freaked when you found out I was a vampire."

Dad looked surprised at that revelation.

"What did you think I was talking about?" I asked suspiciously.

"I thought you'd hate me because of the oral surgery. I was the one who recommended Dr. Bennett take out your canines and now you can't, you know, *feed*. Because of me, you might starve to death!"

To be honest, I hadn't given the lack of fangs much thought up to that point. Since I'd managed to have a, um, light snack earlier, I wasn't hungry but now that my dad brought it up—how *was* I going to eat, anyway?

"Daddy, I don't blame you for not having any fangs. I mean, how could you know I would need them later in life? You just wanted me to have a perfect smile."

My father nodded, looking somewhat relieved.

"I don't want you to think I left the house because I couldn't handle what happened to you. I mean, yes, it is a shock but honey, we didn't know where you were and thought the worst." He shivered. "That was awful. I was just so happy you were with us again. Your mother told me about your fangs and I thought, well, I thought maybe I could help you there."

A little sensation of dread started at the back of my neck and raised the fine hairs.

"What do you mean, Dad?"

"Well, I went to the office and reviewed your last teeth molds. You know the ones we made so you could have a bleaching tray?"

I nodded, still remembering the gaggy melon-flavored gel I used to keep my smile bright.

He put a small box on the bed next to me.

"This is what I came up with."

I eyed the box warily.

"Dad, there isn't a pair of fangs in there, is there? I mean, you didn't make me a pair of ceramic fangs to walk around in, right?"

What was worse than a vampire not having fangs? How about one who had them all the time, not just when they were feeding?

"No, no. I wouldn't know where to start in creating ones that stayed sharp enough to feed but then would retract when you weren't using them. No, no, this will work much better for your needs. Go ahead, open it up." Apparently, he had given this a lot of thought.

I pulled myself into a sitting position and picked up the box. One look at his face told me he was quite proud of this invention and couldn't wait for me to open it. Now I was *sure* I wanted nothing to do with the little container and its contents.

Taking a deep breath, I opened it.

Puzzled, I said, "Looks like my old headgear."

"Precisely!" He pulled out the apparatus to show me. "I created a new upper retainer with stainless-steel fangs. It hooks to your headgear in two places so it stays secure. Then, when you're done, you just pop it off and voilà, no one is the wiser."

I could feel my mouth hanging open and tried to close it. A fang headgear set. As if life wasn't hard enough for me, now I would be the laughingstock of vampires everywhere.

"Here, let's try it on." Dad gave me the retainer, which I dutifully slipped into place. Crap, a perfect fit. Then he adjusted the headgear so a band went behind my neck and over my head. The straps met on either side of my face and slid into the metal plate of my retainer. He grabbed the mirror sitting on my bed to show me his handiwork.

It took all my control not to scream at the reflection. Attempting a smile into the mirror, I caught a flash of silver. I opened wide and closed again. It was a nice snug fit, without any gapping. I experimented with chomping a couple of times. As hideous as it was, it just might work for eating out. But I couldn't possibly wear it in public, could I? Wasn't starving better than being caught in this thing? I mean, wasn't it?

"Dad, I own't know what to shay. I'sh really shomshing." I had a lisp! I struggled not to burst into tears then and there.

"I know it isn't the most fashionable thing but when the time comes, it should work out."

Dad stood up. He took one last look at me in the headgear and nodded. "Yep, it just might do the trick. I'm going to try to get a couple hours of sleep before morning. I love you, angel."

"I luff you shooo, Dad." I took another look at myself in

the mirror after he left, staring in horror. My tongue kept running over the strange appliance in my mouth, trying to get familiar with it. I ran my finger over one of the fangs and cried out in surprise. I looked at my finger and saw a pinprick of blood. The fangs were sharp. Very sharp. I carefully removed the headgear and fell back on the bed. As the sun started to rise and the day began, I couldn't help praying for a good old-fashioned wooden stake to put me out of my misery.

Four

I slept like the dead, if you can pardon the pun. I awoke sometime before dinner, the once mouthwatering scent of pot roast and tiny red potatoes wafting into my room, bringing me slowly to my senses. Stretching like a cat, I enjoyed the aroma of Monday night dinner but didn't have the salivating anticipation I once did. My mom made the best pot roast and I was suddenly angry that I could no longer enjoy it.

If I'd known that my last meal was going to be a side of brown rice at the local teriyaki stand I would have rethought my order. I was now on a permanent liquid diet and the killer was, I doubted I would be able to lose those remaining six pounds. Oh, the injustice of it all!

I changed into jeans and a sweater, pulled my hair back with a clip and grabbed a pair of retro FosterGrants. The big frames made me feel as though I were a famous Somebody trying to escape the paparazzi unrecognized. That sounded much better than Newly Undead Nightstalker hiding funky yellow eyeballs.

I loped down the stairs and stopped short on the bottom step. Mom, Dad and Aunt Chloe were just sitting down to dinner.

"Why didn't you call me down?" I was annoyed they hadn't waited for me. Dinnertime—except when practice and games interfered—was sacred family time, no excuses were accepted, and they'd started without me?

"You were sleeping so peacefully, dear, I didn't want to disturb you. You've had such a rough time," Mom said.

I sniffed and made my way to the table. I was somewhat mollified by my mother's excuse but still, I was a vampire, not a porcelain doll. I wasn't going to break if woken up to join the family for dinner.

I sat in my usual spot and marveled at the amount of food Mom prepared.

"Isn't this a little overkill for the four of us?" I asked skeptically.

"Yes, a little," Mom replied, a bit embarrassed. "It's just so many people came by yesterday when you were still missing and dropped off food. The fridge is overflowing."

I used to wonder why people brought food to families who suffered a tragedy, but not anymore. Who wants to cook dinner when their daughter was missing, possibly dead?

"Well, it looks great," I said and meant it. I really, really meant it. And I couldn't have any of it.

I shoved back from the table in a fit of self-pity. "I'm gonna go watch some TV."

I sullenly stomped to the family room and turned on the television, blatantly disregarding the no-TV rule during family dinner. Mom was having none of it.

"Colby," she said in a warning tone.

"Oh all right, fine! I'll go in the other room." I snapped off the TV. Jeez, you'd think dying would buy you some small privileges, but noooooo.

I went to the formal living room with the stiff, ceremonial furniture and plopped down. Instead of watching the boob tube, I started thumbing through a fashion magazine. I was a quarter of the way through "How to get that special someone to ask you out" when someone knocked on the door.

I jumped up to answer it, ready to invite one of the well-wishing looky-lous in to convince them I was really fine when I stopped at the door and sniffed the air. Something didn't seem right. Sure, the delicious aroma of pot roast still hung in our house but I detected something else. Something sweeter, like chocolate chip cookies.

Great, someone has brought over more food I can't eat. I wrenched the door open with a little more force than intended and it almost flew off the hinges. I was shocked, and it must have shown on my face because the visitors at the door gave each other a very strange look.

"Can I help you?" I asked them, not recognizing either gentleman or spotting a single plate of yummies.

"We're looking for Colby Blanchard," the guy closest to me said. He was around five-eleven with a wiry body, like a soccer player. Not like Aidan's imposing muscles, but he still looked strong and cute. Green eyes and brown hair, cut short in the back and sides, but longer in the bangs. Very retro.

He was maybe eighteen or nineteen, dressed in a button-down shirt, dress slacks and name badge, identifying himself as Thomas from The Tribunal Group. His partner was dressed in a similar fashion and was also handsome, with dark hair and eyes. He was a bit larger and older. His badge said his name was Carl.

"I'm Colby," I said without inviting them in or opening the door wider. They looked just like Evangelics looking to convert and I really didn't have the heart to kindly say I wasn't interested. They must have heard I was back safe and thought I would be an easy target to scare into their religion because of my recent brush with death. Ha! They were a little late. Maybe I should just tell them I was a vampire and see how fast they ran away from the crazy girl in the sunglasses.

They exchanged another glance and Thomas took out a business card, handing it to me. I took it without looking and stared at him, somewhat rudely, which wasn't very nice. But hey, my family was eating *pot roast* and I couldn't have any. That wasn't nice either.

"May we come in?" he asked politely.

"I don't think so," I said, equally politely, causing Carl to scowl at me. Thomas, on the other hand, seemed somewhat amused.

"Something funny?" I asked nastily. Boy, I was just a witch when I was denied food.

"Not at all. You're just not what I expected," he surprised me by saying.

"Who are you guys?" My eyes narrowed behind the dark frames.

"We represent the Tribunal and are here to evaluate your new status." Carl spoke up for the first time. He had a slight Spanish accent and I wondered if Carl was short for Carlos. Either way, it was pretty sexy.

"And what status would that be?" I asked, feigning disinterest. It was the lamest line to check out a local religion I ever heard.

"Your Undead status, of course," Thomas said, gently pushing the door aside and brushing past me.

It took a moment to get my wits together and by then it was too late. Both Carl and Thomas were seated on our uncomfortable green brocade couch, looking at me expectantly.

I decided to gracefully collapse in the chair opposite them and blurt out, "How did you know *that*?"

Yes, I am so cool under pressure.

"Miss Blanchard? May I call you Colby? Yes? Colby then, we are here to ascertain the circumstances surrounding your new status and deal with the situation accordingly." Carl was very smooth but I didn't like the way he said "deal with it."

"What do you want to know?" I asked suspiciously.

"Everything," Carl replied.

"Hmmm, that's a pretty tall order. I'll make you a deal: I'll tell you my story if you answer my questions. Sound fair?"

"I'm afraid it doesn't work that way, Colby. We ask the questions and you answer them." Carl was perhaps the most arrogant hottie I'd ever met, but he had no idea who he was dealing with.

I leaned forward, keeping eye contact with Carl. "Carl? May I call you Carl? You are in my house, uninvited I might add, so turn down the testosterone and turn up the charm because getting high-handed is the fastest road to getting nowhere with me there is."

I smiled pleasantly, sliding my sunglasses down my nose so he could see my eyes for good measure.

"Where are your fangs?" Thomas said, surprising all of us.

"Not showing, Thomas. Now, my turn. What is the Tribunal and are you two vampires?"

They looked at each other. Then Carl opened his mouth to get all uppity again, but Thomas stopped him.

"Colby, both Carl and I are vampires. The Tribunal is a clan of vampires who live in this area."

Now we were getting somewhere.

"Great, how do I meet other vampires? What is the deal about sunlight, wooden stakes, holy water—"

Thomas's laughter interrupted me. "Colby, it's my turn to ask you a question, remember?"

I looked at both Thomas and Carl, who was now stewing in his juices.

"Of course, Thomas, how rude of me. Please, ask your question." I stuck my tongue out at Carl for good measure.

Thomas coughed and I thought for sure he did it to cover more laughter. Carl was pretty sexy but it was Thomas who completely captured my attention.

"What happened the night you became Undead?" I noticed he never used the word "vampire," but maybe that was one of those rules I didn't know about yet. Like being politically correct. *No dear, you never call them vampires. They prefer the term "Undead."*

"I was walking home after a game Friday night and some guy called my name and stopped me. He tried to kiss me but I told him no, then we struggled and he threw me down." I was getting emotional again and took a steadying breath. "He bit my neck and I fought him, then he threw me in the ravine. I woke up two days later and here I am."

"That's all that happened?" Carl asked.

As hot as Carl was, he was ticking me off.

"Not enough detail for you, Carl? Were you hoping for a little more"—I wiggled my eyebrows upward—"action?"

Carl actually growled at me and rose so I jumped up as well. Thomas put a restraining hand on Carl's forearm and we both slowly returned to our chairs.

I had no idea what was getting into me. Carl was huge. I was the top of the cheer pyramid, for crying out loud. Did I really think I could take on Carl? This whole Undead thing was really distorting my perceptions of my own abilities.

"Colby, what we are trying to figure out is how you were

changed. What you describe would not change a human into an Undead." My eyes narrowed at him. "Which clearly you are," Thomas added quickly upon seeing my look.

I glanced toward the hallway to make sure my parents weren't listening.

"Okay, he did one other thing. He—he may have made me drink his blood." I said it quickly and winced at the reaction I figured would be coming.

"Ahh, now that makes sense," Carl said, nodding in satisfaction.

I was surprised that they seemed satisfied with my tale now and decided I'd earned the right to ask another question.

"Okay, my turn. Can you only drink blood and can you be killed by a silver bullet?"

Thomas answered, "Yes, we drink blood, but we can also drink water or tea."

I waited for more and when I realized they weren't going to say any more, I prompted, "And?"

"And I have matched you question for question. It's my turn again."

"Oh man, you totally cheated!" I cried out.

"Hello? Evil nightstalker, remember?" Thomas said, pointing to himself and I laughed. I could appreciate a good trick.

"Fine, next question."

"Can you show me your fangs?"

I stood up and turned to leave. He interrupted, "Where are you going? If you can't do it, just tell me."

"I can do it, just wait a second. Sheesh." I ran upstairs and grabbed the box with my headgear. I quickly returned and was met with looks of surprise. "What?"

"You are remarkably fast for an Undead," Thomas commented.

"Oh, am I? I guess I hadn't noticed. Here you go." I tossed him the box.

"What is this?" he asked.

I rolled my eyes. "My fangs. You asked to see them, remember?"

Thomas opened the box doubtfully and pulled the headgear out by the hot pink straps that were stamped with the word "Princess" over and over.

They both looked at the retainer and then at me.

"I'll show you." I grabbed them and slipped my fangs in. Then I strapped the headgear tethers in place.

"Ta-da."

I struck a pose with both of my hands in the air as though I just finished a difficult stunt.

Carl turned a kind of molten red and jumped to his feet, exclaiming, "You dare mock us?!" He reached across the coffee table with amazing speed but I saw him coming. I slapped his hand aside and pushed him back with all my might. He went flying into the couch and the whole thing slammed into the wall.

My family came running into the living room when they heard the crash. I quickly removed my fangs.

"Colby? What happened?" Dad demanded as he entered the room, Mom and Aunt Chloe hot on his heels.

"Oh, we have guests," Mom said awkwardly, as they took in the scene in front of them. It must have looked pretty odd to see two strange guys sitting on a couch that was now partly embedded into the wall.

"I'll make some tea," Aunt Chloe offered.

"Don't bother, they were just leaving," I said, moving to stand in front of my family as I gestured to the door.

Thomas was astute enough to take it as their cue to leave. He stood up and pulled a packet of papers from behind his back. They must have been tucked into his waistband.

"These are for you. Read them and if you have any questions, my number is on the card."

He walked Carl to the door and I made sure I was always between them and my family. When they exited, I walked to the still open door and called out in a falsetto, "So nice of you to stop by. Give my best to the wife and kids."

I carefully shut the door and locked it.

"Who was that, Colby?" my dad asked in shock.

"That was the Vampire Welcome Wagon."

Five

"They didn't act so welcoming," my aunt murmured.

"Yeah, not so much," I agreed and patted her shoulder reassuringly.

"What did he give you, honey?" Mom wanted to know. For that matter, so did I.

"I hope it's a vampire user manual or something, but I'm not sure." I opened it up and pulled out a bunch of official-looking documents that were notarized. Vampires had notaries?

I started to skim the letter, then slowed down to read it more carefully.

"What is it?" my mother insisted.

"It's a summons. I am being called to some sort of vampire court."

"Whatever for?" Aunt Chloe asked.

"Apparently, I am Undead without a license."

"That's the most ridiculous thing I have ever heard—"

"What?! That's insane—"

"Is that like traffic court for vampires?"

They all spoke at once.

I handed the paperwork to my mother, who was used to legal jargon and such. I sat down in the chair I'd occupied earlier, my head swirling with the information I'd just read.

"Colby, you know what this means, don't you?" my mother asked seriously.

"Yeah, Mom. In three days I have to go before the Tribunal board and defend my existence. If I can't, I will be 'relieved of my Undead status.'"

"My, that doesn't sound good," Aunt Chloe said to no one in particular.

Nope, it didn't sound good at all.

After the Tribunal dropped its little bombshell on us, I wasn't in the mood for any other visitors. Our family needed to have an emergency meeting. But alas, the well-wishers just started rolling in.

Marci and Rachel gushed over me when they stopped by, which did a lot to boost my spirits.

"Ohmigod! You poor thing. Are you okay?"

"What happened?! Tell us everything! Are you sure you're okay?"

I retold the same version my mother shared with the police, including my clumsy trip into the ravine.

"You are so lucky you're a bit of a klutz, Colby. I mean he could've killed you or worse!" Rachel's eyes were as big as plates and I couldn't help wonder what was worse than being dead in her eyes. Being Undead?

"She's right, you know. Stumbling during a stunt just embarrasses you in front of the whole school, but stumbling down the hill *saved your life*!" They both nodded in unison.

I wasn't that klutzy, was I?

"Why are you wearing sunglasses?" Marci demanded, trying to remove them. I shooed her hands away.

"Black eyes, I don't want to gross you guys out."

"It's okay, we don't mind. We're your friends." Rachel looked only too pleased to see my phantom injury but I held firm. What would they do if they discovered I was really hiding yellow eyes? I imagined Rachel's first concern would be accessorizing with the appropriate matching shadow.

They didn't stay long once they realized I had nothing new to share. I stood at the door, assuring them as they climbed into their car that I would see them later on.

"You're not going to school tomorrow," Mom announced, coming toward me.

"Why not?"

"School can wait a couple days until we figure out what we are going to do. How do you expect to go to class when you sleep all day? We have to go to the police station and make an official statement. No, no. You're staying home for awhile."

I still held the door open as I started to complain, "Mom, I can't miss school. What about cheering? What about my classes? I have that college interview coming up, midterms to prep for. I can't just hang out at home."

"I'll get your homework." Piper surprised me by sliding through the door and greeting my mother with a container of baked goods.

"See? It's all settled. Piper will get your schoolwork, cheering can wait, and you can go back to school when you are physically ready."

I glared at Piper as Mom went back to the kitchen.

"Well, aren't you helpful." My voice dripped sarcasm.

"Good to see your ordeal hasn't changed the sweet Colby we all know and love," Piper retorted.

I sighed deeply. Piper was right—she was just trying to help and I was being a brat.

"I'm sorry, Piper. Thanks for offering to bring me my homework."

Piper shook her head as though she couldn't believe her ears. She even went so far as to try to clean them out with her finger.

"Ha, ha," I said, smiling.

"Maybe you fell harder than we all thought."

"Klutzy me," I said with a self-deprecating smile.

"You're not klutzy. If some nut job surprised me on the trail, I would have fallen down the ravine too. Just be thankful you're okay."

"Thanks. Do you wanna sit down?" Too late I remembered the sofa embedded in the wall.

She lifted an eyebrow. "Rearranging the furniture?"

"Uh, we had a little accident. Follow me."

I led her into the kitchen, where Mom had left the plate of cookies on the table.

"Try these. They're great," Piper said, popping a piece in her mouth.

"Maybe later," I said, eyeing them longingly.

"It wouldn't kill you to eat a cookie now and then, Colby."

Fat lot she knew.

"It's not that. I just can't seem to keep much down with my concussion and all. I guess it's pretty common."

"Dude, I'm sorry. That was real insensitive of me."

I felt bad for lying to her but what was I going to say? Sorry, I can only have blood cookies, the chocolate ones make me hurl?

"Listen, I'll let you get some rest." She stood up from the barstool and started to back away when Aunt Chloe entered the kitchen.

"Colby, I have a friend who volunteers at the blood bank. I think I can get us a couple of pints to see if you can drink it out of the bag and then you won't have to use those fangs your father made you."

I froze. Piper froze. But Aunt Chloe just kept talking.

"He means well, bless his heart, but you can't be expected to feed wearing that silly headgear. What would the other vampires say if they saw you? You can hardly defend your existence if everyone knows you don't have real fangs, now can you?"

I was horrified. Aunt Chloe simply hadn't seen Piper and there was no way I could explain away what she was talking about.

Aunt Chloe finally realized someone else was in the room with us.

"Oh, hello there. Are you one of Colby's vampire friends?" To be fair, looking at Piper with her pale skin, lined eyes and many facial accessories, she made a pretty strong case for mistaken identity.

Piper wasn't sure what to say. She stood there kind of gaping at me.

"No, Aunt Chloe, Piper is a friend from school. She lives next door," I said.

"Oh, that's just as well, dear. Do you really think it's a good idea to go telling all your friends you're really a vampire? You should probably keep it a secret." She *tsked* at me, as though Piper knowing my true identity was entirely my fault, and left the room.

Piper and I looked at each other awkwardly. I didn't know what to say and neither, apparently, did she.

"Look—"

"What—"

We both spoke at the same time.

"You go first," I said, expecting all sorts of freaked-out questions and hysteria.

"What happened to your fangs?"

I blinked twice at her. Piper wasn't freaking out and she seemed to take what my aunt said at face value.

Now it was my turn to be flustered. "Uh, well, I had them removed. When I was twelve. For braces."

Piper nodded knowingly. My father was also her orthodontist.

"Why do you have to defend your existence?"

"I'm not licensed. You have to have a vampire license to be a vampire."

"Why don't you have a license?"

"Because I didn't know I was going to become a vampire."

"Makes sense to me."

We both nodded in agreement.

"So, how'd it happen?" Piper finally asked and I started to laugh. Apparently, *nothing* fazed Piper. She joined in and we both sat down at the table and I told her the truth about my attack.

"So these guys just showed up earlier tonight and gave you a summons to go to vampire court? That's really bizarre." She sat across from me, munching contently on cookies and milk.

"I know, it's like, hello? I didn't ask to be Undead. Can't I get off with a warning or something?"

"Do you think those other girls were changed into vampires too? Especially that last girl who said she was knocked down. Sounds a lot like your story, don't you think?"

"Hey, I didn't even think about that! When was she attacked?" I got up and checked the recycling bin that had last week's papers in it.

"Here it is. Look, this last article has the days of the

attacks. There. That's the last attack. Wow, that was almost a week ago."

"Maybe she needs to get her license too?"

I nodded in agreement.

"I wonder if there's some way to find out who she is. They don't list her name."

"It says she goes to Newport. That can't be too hard to figure out. Between both of us, we've got to know someone at Newport who would know."

We both tried to think of anyone we could call but came up blank. Anyone sports-related I knew, I didn't have their full name or contact info. Anyone Piper knew, she only had a nickname and didn't know their real name. She did see people in chat rooms who might go to Newport but when she logged on at our kitchen computer, they weren't online.

"I'll just keep checking the chat rooms until I can get the scoop. So why are you wearing those sunglasses?" she asked me.

I took them off and explained about my skin and eyes.

"Too weird. How are you going to hide them? You can't wear sunglasses in class, you know. For that matter, if you're a vampire, don't you need to sleep during the day?"

"Well, I am able to go out in sunlight, believe it or not. I'm going to try to stay awake during the day tomorrow. I was thinking I might be able to wear colored contacts."

"Do you have any?" she asked.

"Yeah, I don't need glasses but I have contacts to enhance the blue in my eyes. I just haven't tried them since I changed."

She jumped up. "What are you waiting for? Come on."

We went upstairs to my bedroom and I tried the contact lenses. Piper was slowly doing the rounds in my room, mocking my shaggy pink bedspread and playing with my pom-poms.

"Cut it out, will you? How do they look?"

She walked closer to examine them.

"Still too light. They look bright green." I guess when you mix yellow with blue you really do get green.

"You need those opaque contact lenses to completely disguise the yellow."

I sat down at my vanity and started a list.

—get new contacts
—buy self-tanner

"Buy self-tanner?" Piper questioned.

"Yeah, I'm not walking around like some chalky zombie. I need my color."

I continued with the list.

—new makeup to match complexion

"What else?" I said.

"I don't know. What else do vampires need?" She started roaming around my room again, stopping at my window and peeking out.

"Uh, Colby. Who's that?" she said, pointing.

I got up and looked. Standing in my driveway was my

attacker. He was wearing the same clothes as the night he turned me into a vampire.

"I"—I cleared my throat—"I'm not sure. Do you recognize him?"

"Yeah, kind of. I think I've seen him at school. Just can't seem to think of where. Detention? Or maybe he lives around here?"

I was trembling slightly so I moved away from the window and sat down on the bed.

"Are you okay? You're not going to faint from lack of blood, are you?"

I shook my head to assure her I was fine, but I was anything but. My attacker knew where I lived and he was outside my house at this moment. I just didn't know what to do.

"Piper, I just remembered I have to make a phone call. Do you think we could talk about this tomorrow?"

"Yeah, sure. No problem. And don't worry, I won't tell anyone. Promise."

It just occurred to me that Piper would need to go outside to get home. Outside where my attacker was waiting.

"Thanks. Let me walk you home."

"I don't need an escort, Colby. I just live next door."

"Yeah, I know, but I kind of want to get out of the house. Get a little cool air. Do you mind?"

"Oh. No. I guess not."

We walked downstairs together and I braced myself to look out the window again before we left. There was no sign of my attacker.

I walked Piper home quickly and she promised to stop by after school with my homework. I breathed a sigh of relief when she entered her house safe and sound. I walked slowly around her yard, checking behind the large boat in her side yard, next to my house and peeking around the white picket fence that separated our properties. Satisfied no one was lurking, I crossed her driveway and entered my front yard. The scent of day-old bread filled my nostrils.

"I know you're here. So come out all ready." A slight breeze kicked up and a dog barked down the street. Other than that, it was quiet.

"Fine, you want to play games. We'll play games. I spy with my little eye . . ."

He materialized behind me in a flash and touched my shoulder. I turned to face him.

"Someone who is dead."

Six

"Hello, Colby. Surprised to see me?" He smiled in delight, like a child who was allowed to play with a school chum an extra hour.

I stood my ground and repeated "He can't hurt me" in my head until I felt myself relax a little. He'd done his worst to me and I was still here, so I let go of the rest of my fear.

"Who are you and what do you want?" I was surprised how annoyed I sounded. At least I didn't sound scared, which was how I thought it would come out.

"Oh, forgive me. Where are my manners? We have not been formally introduced." He bowed with flourish, as though we were meeting in a renaissance courtyard and not in a modern-day cul-de-sac.

"I am Lord Charles Winthrop, at your service, and the

reason I am here should be obvious. I have come to take you home."

"Oookay then. Listen, Chuck—"

"The name is Charles."

"Whatever. Listen, I'm not going anywhere with you."

He seemed genuinely surprised. "But we're family! My family has always lived together."

"Dude, I already have a family. And the guy who bit me and threw me into the ravine is not a part of it, get me?"

"I'm sorry about losing my temper and throwing you into that gully. I was angered that you struggled so. But my dear Colby, we are family. I am your Creator and your allegiance is to me."

"Wow, you are so not getting it. You're not my anything. I don't know you, I don't like you and I have a family who loves and cares for me. So take a hike. Beat it."

He was getting angry again, but then so was I. How dense did he have to be? I was never going to hang with him, ever. Couldn't he see that?

"I'm afraid this won't do at all," he said through clenched teeth. He looked at my house and caught a brief glimpse of Great-Aunt Chloe walking by the window.

"Don't even think about it," I said in my most menacing tone. "You get within so much as ten feet of anyone in my family, I will stake you so fast it will make your head spin."

He laughed at me, so full of self-assurance. "Dearest Colby, you wouldn't hurt me."

I stepped closer, until we were practically nose to nose,

which meant Chuck was not all that tall. I looked deep into his eyes, making sure I had his complete attention, and whispered, "Watch me."

His face lost all amusement. He growled and tried to slap me but I was too fast. I dodged his blow and kicked him in the groin, again. He buckled forward, gasping.

"I wish you would quit *doing* that," he said with a moan.

"I meant what I said, Chuck. Stay away from me and stay away from my family or your immortal days are over." I started to leave.

"Do you really think those Tribunal Investigators are going to help you, Colby?" he managed to get out.

Despite myself, I turned back to him.

"Oh yes, I know all about Thomas and Carl. They have been chasing me for awhile now. They are never going to give you one of these." He held out his hand and showed me a large old-fashioned ring that looked a lot like a class ring.

"What's that?"

He laughed at my naïveté. "Why, it's what you need, my dear. It's the reason you *will* live with me."

"Why do you want me to come with you so badly? And don't give me the family line again. I know families who are glad to live hundreds of miles from each other."

He stared at me hard. "You are different. You are strong. There is something special about you."

He turned to leave. "And, Colby, dear? Kick me again and I will rip off your leg." He said it so casually I shivered. Then he disappeared in the light fog that was always present in the autumn evenings in our neighborhood on the Plateau.

As if in a daze, I walked back inside my house and straight up to my room. I picked up Thomas's card, took a deep breath and dialed the number. He picked up on the first ring.

"Thomas here."

"Hello? This is—"

"Colby Blanchard."

Well really, who else would it be?

"Yes, I was wondering if maybe you and I could talk a little more about, well, uh, about my circumstances."

"Sure. Shall we say about an hour from now?"

Wow, that was quick.

"Great, how about we meet at the Krispy Kreme at the bottom of the hill from my house?"

"Are you sure you want to meet in public?" he asked uncertainly.

"Actually, I insist on it. Oh, and no Carl please."

He chuckled into the phone and my toes curled in pleasure.

"That would be fine. See you then."

I caught a glimpse of myself in the mirror as I put down the phone. I was smiling! I was completely crushing on this guy—this *vampire*. I had to snap out of it. The last time we spoke his buddy wanted to kill me, and the only other vampire I knew was the nut job who wanted to be my family but also threatened to tear off my leg. I had no reason to assume that Thomas wasn't just as whacked-out as the rest of them.

Still, I dressed with extra care. Low-slung jeans, turtle-neck sweater, cute half boots and matching scarf. It said "interested" without trying that hard. I added a swipe of pink lip gloss with blusher, popped on my FosterGrants and was out the door with time to spare.

I borrowed the car from Dad with only a short amount of resistance. Once I mentioned feeding, he couldn't give me the keys fast enough. He was dying to know how his invention would hold up to practical application. He even wanted to come along but I convinced him I couldn't eat with anyone else watching. I was too self-conscious. It must have been the oddest conversation between daughter and father in the history of mankind.

When I arrived at the Krispy Kreme, the parking lot was pretty deserted. It was more of a hangout on Friday and Saturday nights, but on Monday things were pretty lame. I waited in my car until exactly the appointed time. I opened the door and was overwhelmed by the scent of doughnuts, which normally would have been a good thing. But with my new olfactory superpowers, I wasn't sure this was the best place to meet Thomas after all.

He arrived right after me, dressed in a forest green sweater that hugged his shoulders (yum) and faded, fitted jeans (yum, yum) that hugged his thighs. Seeing Thomas in 501's made me want to ban baggy pants from the face of the earth. I was pretty into him and somehow, I didn't care that he was a vampire. After all, so was I.

"Hey," I said as he slipped into the booth across from me.

"How are you doing?" he asked, his eyes reflecting concern. "This can't be very easy for you."

And the prize for understatement of the year goes to . . . the hunky vampire in the doughnut shop.

"Well, I admit it isn't easy finding out you're a vampire."

"Colby, you're not a vampire."

Seven

"Excuse me? Then why do I drink blood?"

"Colby, you're Undead, but not a vampire."

"Is this because I don't have a license yet? Because I can't officially call myself a vampire without it?"

"No—you aren't fully Blooded, that's why you can't call yourself a vampire. You are too many generations removed from the original vampires to actually *be* one."

"I don't understand."

"Your attacker, Charles Winthrop, is a fully Blooded vampire, but we estimate he is twelfth or thirteenth generation. We aren't entirely sure, but we do know his offspring are not fully Blooded. Mongrels, if you will."

I'm not a vampire?! I'm a half-blooded mongrel?! Oh, I don't think so.

"So even though you have vampire characteristics, you are not a true vampire," Thomas finished.

"I see. Tell me what characteristics a true vampire has."

"Well, we can't go in the sunlight; are burned by holy water; must feed daily; have superhuman strength, speed and hearing. Also, we have a finely tuned sense of smell, and we are immortal."

"That's it in a nutshell then?"

He smiled at my comment.

"Do half-bloods tend to have some of the characteristics?" I asked.

"Yes, they can have any combination but never at the same capacity of a Blooded vampire."

"Probably gives you Blooded guys a feeling of real superiority over us poseurs, huh?" I said it teasingly, but he nodded as though I was serious.

"We *are* superior—and there are no other half-bloods. The license process ensures that no genetic mutants are created."

Genetic mutants?! No one calls me a genetic mutant, no matter how hot they look in jeans!

"Seems like your vampire license process just doesn't work," replied the resentful genetic mutant half-blood.

He nodded in agreement.

"Occasionally a vampire goes rogue. They can't handle the new system; it's too much for them. They become unstable and want to start their own clan."

"How new is this system?" I envisioned a process that was still so young, a lot of the vampires weren't ready to adapt.

"Only about two hundred years old."

Wow!

"How long have you been a vampire?"

"I was turned during the war."

I didn't want to sound stupid but if the law was considered young at 200 years old, then Thomas could be referring to any number of wars. Human history was jam-packed with them.

"Which war?"

"World War Two."

So he was around eighty years old, give or take a few. It wasn't fair that gramps here still looked like a college boy and now that I knew his real age, I was *still* infatuated with him. Was I creepy or what?

I looked down at his hands. Sure enough, he was wearing a ring similar to Chuck's but not nearly as old. I played dumb. "What's that?"

"My license." He held his hand out for me to see.

"Can I hold it?"

He smiled. "Sorry, it only comes off when I'm dead."

"Eek," I muttered, looking it over across the table. "Looks old."

"Not really. I am relatively young. I didn't have a license in the beginning either, you know."

Now that was intriguing. "Really? Tell me about it."

"I was stationed in Germany, in the war. We marched on Normandy and during the fighting I was separated from my unit. I was terrified, I'm not ashamed to tell you. Anyway, I was hiding until daylight so I could find my unit without getting shot by patrols when this German soldier is suddenly right next to me. I didn't hear a thing. I thought for sure I was a goner. It was odd he didn't reach for a weapon. No gun, no knife, nothing. I was struggling to get my gun when he told me to stop, and I did. I just looked at him and was filled with numbness. I couldn't move. He told me to look at the stars and I did, then he fed upon me."

I was transfixed by his story, remembering the sensation of numbness but also remembering that I was able to fight it off.

Thomas continued, "When he drank his fill, I was barely alive. I don't know why he did it, but he opened his own vein and made me drink. He created me."

"What happened then?" I was fully enraptured with his story, so parallel to my own.

"I passed out and woke up a couple hours later. The soldier was still with me. I had an unbearable thirst and he seemed to understand this. He took me to a place where I could feed."

"Where was that?" I asked.

Thomas's gaze hardened a little, but he answered my question. "He took me to a battleground where most of the men were already dead. I found one or two that were too far gone to save."

"I'm so sorry, Thomas. That must have been terrible for you."

For a moment he seemed lost in thought but shook himself out of it when I asked, "How did you finally get your license?"

"At the time, Germany had its own Princes and were

adopting the license procedure, though it worked a little differently. I brought them the license of my Creator and I was given his license as my own."

"So you had to kill him, right? That was the only way you could get his license."

"Yes."

"I don't understand. Why did he do it? He had his license. Wasn't he getting along just fine?"

Thomas sighed deeply. "My Creator had been a vampire for hundreds of years. That does something to you. He was very sick. You will learn that vampires don't live in the human world but my Creator was in the army, living with other humans. It does something to the mind. Makes you dream impossible dreams."

Okay, whatever that means. He didn't seem to want to talk about it anymore so I changed the subject. "So why get a license at all? Why is it necessary?"

"It's the law. It's due process. Listen, Colby, there was a time when our kind was primal and savage. There were tribal feuds for power and many vampires lost their lives. Despite this, no one wanted to create more offspring for fear their children would usurp their power and kill them. Our kind was on the brink of extinction. It took the creation of the Tribunal to save us. Other areas began to adapt our notion and slowly we are rebuilding our race."

"So the Tribunal is what? The vampire congress or something?"

"The Tribunal of any area consists of the three most

powerful vampires, or Princes, to use an old-school term. They govern our area and keep the peace."

"Why three and not just one?"

"Balance of power. When there is only one Prince, it is a monarchy. Two Princes means a complete deadlock if they don't agree in all decisions; nothing gets accomplished. Three Princes gives checks and balances. It's the best way to run things smoothly."

It sounded a lot like American democracy to me, and look how easily *that* gets screwed up. "So what do I need to do to get my license?"

Thomas looked slightly uncomfortable with my question, which did nothing to help the growing unease that was making its way up my spine. He thought a moment before answering. "You must present a solid argument for why you should live in the vampire world. Define the value you bring to the community."

"Would it help if I told them I didn't plan to live in the vampire world? I mean, I'm going to live with my parents for now, then college, get a good job and go from there."

Thomas shook his head at me. "I told you, vampires do not live in the human world. We have our own society."

"You are mixing in the human world right now." I pointed out the obvious.

"That is different. It is my job to seek out the unlicensed and investigate their existence. All vampires enter the human world to feed but they don't live there. Do you see the difference?"

I guess I could see his point. It was like stopping at Mc-Donald's to grab lunch. Everybody did it but nobody would say they lived there.

My thoughts must have shown on my face because Thomas reached over and touched my hand. I felt a warm and tingly sensation go up my arm and through my body all the way down to my toes. Aidan never made me feel like this.

"Let me help you, Colby. You are very strong for a half-blood. You possess more vampire traits than any I have investigated before. With my help, you could make a strong argument for a license in front of the Tribunal."

I stared into his green eyes and might have agreed to anything, especially since he was holding my hand, but a tiny part of me wanted to know why. Why did he want to help me when he obviously had such strong feelings about not pissing in the gene pool, so to speak?

With all the willpower I possessed, I pulled my hand out of his and asked the obvious. "Why do you want to help me? I'm an abomination in your pure vampire eyes. Why not just stake me and call it a day?"

"Because you are different. You're strong. There is something very special about you, Colby Blanchard. I don't know what it is yet; I just know I want to help you."

What girl in her right mind wouldn't swoon at such a speech? If I'd had to stand up at that moment, I knew my legs wouldn't support me. The man was positively *dreamy*. If it wasn't the second time I'd heard such a speech in the span of a couple hours, I was sure I would have done anything Thomas asked me to do.

"I appreciate the offer, I really do. I just don't see what's in it for you."

Thomas looked hurt and I immediately wanted to take it back.

"I don't want to sound ungrateful but come on, Thomas—last time we talked your buddy wanted to rip my head off! My only other contact with vampires has been being attacked and thrown into a ravine. You guys aren't exactly convincing me to put my life in your hands for safekeeping."

"Let me take you to one of *our* places. You can see for yourself that not everyone is like Winthrop."

Was Thomas the hottie vampire asking me out on a date? I pretended to give it some serious thought, when all the while my heart was beating at least three times per minute.

"Fair enough. I'll go."

Thomas wasted no time showing me his world. We left in his car, a '69 Camaro that was obviously his pride and joy. He explained that he'd done most of the restoration himself; before the war he had worked in his father's garage. He was handy with mechanical things and enjoyed discovering the beauty beneath neglected antiques. Not that a '69 car was an antique, he was quick to point out, but still, it seemed pretty old to me.

I was sure I wasn't dressed correctly for a night of vampire clubbing but Thomas assured me I looked fine and wouldn't let me change. Men, they just don't get it. He took us to Old

Town, where most of the quaint little shops had long since closed for the night. Then I noticed a tiny neon sign above a plain black door between a consignment furniture store and an optical shop.

"Ink, huh?" I said, referring to the name of the establishment. He just winked at me and knocked on the door. A small window opened, much like in the old 1920s movies when Prohibition was in its heyday. Thomas held up his license and the door opened for us.

Inside was dark, with soft candlelight gracing tables, walls and chandeliers. It felt very much like an old English pub except a lot of the décor was surprisingly modern, with smooth lines and clutter-free design.

It was a nice combination of the Old World with the New and I felt comfortable there. Something I never expected.

We sat at a table close to a small stage. The place was half full on this Monday night but Thomas assured me it was standing room only around 3 A.M. I guess when you do all of your living, so to speak, during the evening, 3 A.M. was prime entertainment hour.

"So what happens here?" I asked, nodding in the direction of the stage.

"Plays, bands, dancing. All the usual stuff."

"I notice there are no TVs. Guess all you guy vampires just aren't into sports anymore."

Thomas laughed at me, causing a few heads to turn in our direction. A buzzing of speculative conversation began around us. I thought I heard "mutant," "abomination" and a few other unkind phrases but chose to tune them out. Luckily I hadn't inherited the keen vampire hearing when I was changed and Thomas didn't seem to notice as he answered.

"If you want to watch sports, then you go to Vic's place."

The vampire world wasn't so different from the human world. There were date spots, sports bars and literature especially for bloodsuckers all within the confines of the human world. I was amazed we—that is to say, humans—didn't know what was going on and shared that observation with Thomas.

"We are not so different," he replied. "Our roots are in humanity. We can conform and blend when we must. The older vampires have a harder time blending and in turn they become more isolated."

I thought of Great-Aunt Chloe who had seen two world wars, the invention of plastic revolutionize medicine and all the electronic gadgets she refused to have anything to do with. She didn't leave her community much, but then she lived in Providence Point, where all her neighbors were around her age. They had tons of activities on campus as well as buses to take them everywhere but still, I felt a twinge of sadness for her. It must be hard watching all your friends die and rarely seeing babies and children. Sounded downright depressing. I sighed.

"What's that for?"

"Just thinking how sad it must be for the older vampires. They have seen so many changes in the human world, they aren't comfortable around people anymore, they're all alone.

They remember the days before licenses and must still be paranoid, so they don't hang with their own kind much. Sounds very lonely."

Thomas looked surprised and murmured, "You are an amazingly perceptive person."

When he realized what he said, he turned a delightful shade of red and coughed to cover his embarrassment. If I wasn't careful, I could easily fall for Thomas, despite our nearly seventy-year age difference. The thought made me smile and Thomas took my hand across the table. So we sat there like that, just looking at each other, holding hands and listening to the soft murmur of voices around us.

My stomach felt like a million butterflies were twittering around in it because his hand felt so strong and fit so perfectly with mine.

It was funny. Holding Thomas's hand felt more intimate than kissing any other boy, even Aidan, who I usually hooked up with for some light tonsil action at parties hoping he would ask me out. After all, I wanted a date for Homecoming and he still hadn't asked me, so I thought a little convincing was in order. Now another week passed and I was still dateless.

"What are you thinking about with such intensity?" Thomas asked.

I felt myself blush. Hmm, I could hardly blurt out I was thinking how I'd tried to get another guy to ask me to Homecoming while I was holding hands with him, so I just smiled. "This whole vampire thing. It changes quite a lot for me."

Thomas nodded gravely and slowly pulled his hand out of mine.

"We should use this time to educate you about vampire life."

He was all business and the tender moment we shared was over. I kicked myself for ruining it with thoughts of Aidan.

"Okay. Where do you want to start?"

"Let's start with feeding."

I squirmed a little in my chair and my stomach growled. I was fighting the hunger and thought I could go another day or two without eating, but not if we were going to talk about it.

His eyebrow rose when he heard my stomach again. I widened my eyes in innocence, pretending it wasn't me growling like a wolf.

"You should feed," he said.

"Feed? Nah, I'm good." My stomach growled again and this time I thought I saw the couple next to us look toward me in surprise.

"Colby . . ." Thomas was using his warning tone.

"Listen, Thomas, I'm not like you. I'm not going to go postal and start sucking on everyone here if I don't feed right away. Sure, I could eat but I don't *need* to feed right now."

Thomas sighed heavily, in a way that made his feelings about my stubbornness clear, then raised his hands in defeat. "Okay."

"Let's just talk about something else, okay?" I kind of snapped at him but tried to soften the attack with a smile. All this talk about feeding was making me grumpy.

"Fine, let's talk about your fangs."

I narrowed my stare. "What about them?"

Thomas just looked at me until I finally confessed, "Okay, I had my canine teeth removed when I was twelve, for braces. My dad whipped up these fangs-to-go devices so I can feed, okay?"

Thomas nodded sagely, though I thought I saw a twinkle of amusement in his eye.

"Now I have a question. I want to know about the whole sunlight thing."

"Okay. A vampire sleeps during the day and is active at night."

"Duh. I want to know *why*."

"We are no longer children of the sun. We are night creatures who belong to the darkness. The sun will burn a vampire instantly. It's as simple as that."

"What about sleeping during the day? Do you have to do that?"

"Most vampires sleep during the day but many will awaken for a few hours and stay in the dark, until they can leave the protection of their dens. But most prefer to sleep the entire day. It is safer that way."

"Safer because of the sunlight?"

"Among other things."

"What other things?"

"I don't think we need to get into that now," he hedged.

"So much for telling me about the vampire world. Guess you're only going to tell me what you want me to know and not the full deal, huh?" Being hungry made it easy to dump on Thomas. Also, I was scared about feeding for the first time (I was trying to block out drinking my mom's blood) but it was easier to be nasty than ask for help. Apparently, I had issues.

Thomas quietly looked at me. It wasn't a stare meant to make me feel uncomfortable or contrite for my rude behavior. He truly looked at me. I returned his gaze without flinching or turning away, which was very hard to do. Thomas had a way of looking at me that made me wonder if he could read my mind.

"Let's get out of here," he said abruptly, standing up and practically lifting me out of the chair with him.

Before I could utter a word, we were back out on the street.

He didn't take me to his car. Instead he held my hand and we walked together through Old Town. We came to a large park, complete with a skateboard area where several people were milling about. A few looked downright unsavory, but I didn't feel afraid. Was it because Thomas was at my side or because I knew they couldn't hurt me? I wasn't sure. Either way, I barely spared them a glance as we strolled in the crisp evening, enjoying the unusually clear night and twinkling stars.

We sat down on a bench under a clump of trees that obscured the street light in that part of the park. It was the perfect place to apologize, if I could find the words.

"Put on your headgear," Thomas ordered softly, looking over my shoulder.

Eight

Instead of arguing, I surprised myself and him by obeying without question, glad someone who knew what to do was in charge and grateful he understood my need and at the same time my squeamishness.

"I'm going to leave you alone on this bench and send you someone. They will allow you to feed and then you will leave them. Do you understand?"

I nodded slowly, warring with myself over "feeding" in general. It seemed so wrong, depraved and vicious but I knew from experience it didn't need to be any of those things. In the end it came down to survival.

A few minutes later a woman in her early twenties came to sit down next to me. She was in some sort of trance and I was sure she was under Thomas's vampire mojo spell.

Did he believe for a minute I was going to feed on a woman? What made him think I was going to act out his warped vampire fantasy? I told the girl to go home. She stood up abruptly and continued walking down the path. Suddenly, two guys stepped out of the shadows in front of her. I jumped up when I realized she wasn't aware of them since she was still operating under orders and not thinking for herself.

"Let her pash," I said, surprising them with my stealth.

"Why should we?" one sneered, his tattooed neck exposed by his sweatshirt.

"Becaush you can play with me inshtead." Oh, ya had to love the intimidating lisp I had going.

By this time their original victim was farther up the path. She was still on her way home, not letting anything prevent her from that task.

Both men looked at me in shock. Then they looked at each other when I sighed heavily.

"Guysh, I don't haff all night."

"What are you wearing?" one of them asked.

"Headgear."

"Like braces? Is that why you talk so funny?"

"Kinda like brashesh but more for eating. And I don't talk funny."

"Weird," he said, coming closer for a better look.

I took offense to the weird comment—hey, it wasn't my fault I was fang handicapped—and grabbed him by the collar, lifting him up slightly. He was pretty tall so I couldn't lift him much, but it certainly got his attention.

"Wanna go in the shadowsh for a little bite to eat?" I asked softly, my steel fangs flashing when I spoke.

The guy widened his eyes and tried to speak but I softly shushed him. Then I looked over my shoulder at his buddy who was still in shock seeing me hold up his 200-pound friend.

"You wait here quietly. Don't bother anyone elsh." He nodded his head in agreement, very slowly. I let his buddy down and ordered him to take a few steps back into the shadows.

Once I had my willing victim standing obediently in the shadows with his buddy playing lookout, I was at a loss on how to continue. After all, every vampire movie I ever saw represented nightstalkers in a ruthless, cruel way, toying with their prey, and then devouring them with relish.

In reality, it was a fairly unexciting yet necessary transaction, much like going to the cash machine. I would get sustenance and he would lose a cup of blood, none the wiser. Seemed almost anticlimatic.

I told him to look to the side and show me his neck. He obeyed instantly. I went on tiptoe, barely able to reach, and giggled. Then I giggled some more. My giggling turned into full-fledged hysterical laughter. It must have been the most ridiculous sight to any passerby. A tiny blonde vampire with headgear standing on tiptoes to reach her linebacker prey who was docilely baring his neck to be dinner.

When I finally got hold of myself, I couldn't help noticing the heat radiating from his neck and put my mouth to the pulsing vein. I tentatively bit. My victim stiffened, but did not struggle. The first flow of warm blood flooded my mouth and I opened my throat to drink. It was the sweetest nectar I ever tasted and instantly, I felt alive again. Well, not truly alive but the closest to it since I became Undead. I wish I could have drunk forever but I felt full very quickly so I licked his neck and the wound instantly sealed.

"Uh, shank you," I said very formally, my meal still standing, looking much like a deer in headlights.

I directed my speech to both of them. "You and your buddy need to go shtraight home. You won't remember any of thish but you will be polite to all ladiesh you meet in the park and let them pash. Got it?"

They both nodded dumbly, still staring with unfocused eyes.

I wasn't sure how to continue so I gave a sort of royal wave with my hand and said, "Be gone."

When I was alone or at least thought I was alone the scent of chocolate chip cookies lingered faintly in the fall evening air.

I removed my headgear, wiping it on my jeans to try and remove any traces of leftover blood. I hated the lisp thing. All words with "s" and "v" came out totally lame. Dropping the gear in its box, I methodically placed it back in my bag. Thomas stood next to me. I chose to ignore him and he chose to let me.

I was so conflicted and confused, and felt terribly vulnerable. So this was it. The rest of my life I would be slinking around dark alleys and deserted parks looking for would-be hooligans or confirmed felons to feed upon so I could survive. I fought down a sob, hiccupping instead. I was the most pathetic vampire—no, scratch that, *half-blood* vampire to ever stalk a skate park.

Thomas gently put his arm around me and I sort of melted against him. He turned to hold me, stroking my hair and crooning an old Irish lullabye while I clung to him, sobbing dry tears.

"I hate this! I miss cheeseburgers and milkshakes. I mean, I never ate them because I have to be the top of the pyramid, but if I would have known the last piece of cheesecake I ever had was truly the *last piece of cheesecake* I would have eaten more than one crummy bite!"

Thomas mumbled something into my hair.

"What?"

"I miss Mallomars."

I hiccupped and giggled at the same time. We held each other another moment. Then I said, "You know, I used to suggest going for ice cream after the game and I'd watch everyone else order and when it was my turn I wouldn't indulge. I would just buy bottled water. That way I could watch everyone else eat their ice cream and I'd think to myself I was so much more disciplined than they were.

"What a twit I was. Now what I wouldn't give to go back and order the biggest brownie nut sundae and inhale the whole thing."

"Eating isn't the only thing that is different now, Colby. I don't want to upset you further, but being immortal is . . .

difficult. You will outlive your parents, friends, loved ones, etcetera. Not everyone adjusts."

"It doesn't have to be so hard. I mean, I've met you and surely I'll meet others I get along with. Then it won't be so lonely, right?" I pleaded.

"Colby, there are no other half-bloods. You are alone. I don't want to frighten you, but you must be told. I'm not sure if you heard the murmurs in the tavern, but vampires do not acknowledge or socialize with half-bloods. In their eyes, you should all be destroyed. They won't allow you to intermix with them."

"They let me intermix today," I pointed out.

"That was because you were with an Investigator. The laws as they know it dictate that an Investigator will eliminate half-bloods."

"Well, I don't get it. Why would an Investigator take a half-blood he plans to whack into a tavern?"

"Some Investigators have been known to, uh, toy with half-bloods before eliminating them. It is a practice that is not encouraged, but neither is it condemned."

I wasn't sure what perimeters "toy with" covered, but it sounded bad. Very bad.

"Thomas, are you toying with me?"

"Certainly not! That's an abominable practice left over from the days of savagery," Thomas replied in disgust.

Well, I guess that answered that.

"So, I would be stuck within the human world. That doesn't sound so bad. I mean, I can do that."

"For how long, Colby? Your parents and family will pass on. You will be alone. You will need certain things only the vampire world can give you but you won't be able to get those things easily, since other vampires won't allow half-bloods to buy their goods or services."

I shivered in his arms. "Why are you telling me all this? You make the future sound bleak and miserable."

"We don't even know if you have a future yet, Colby, but forewarned is forearmed."

I looked up into his eyes and asked, "Would you still be around for me? That is, if I'm allowed to . . . ?"

Thomas didn't answer but squeezed me in response. He would stand by me. Right now, in the middle of the night, in Thomas's arms, an eternity of smelling chocolate chip cookies didn't seem like such a rough deal, even if other vampires were dissing me.

"It will be dawn soon. Let me get you home."

We walked back toward his car, his arm slung over my shoulder and mine wrapped around his waist. It would have been a perfect night if it wasn't for the fact that he was a bloodsucking vampire and I was a mutant half-blood who wasn't allowed to exist. But hey, all couples faced some bumps on their way to true love, right?

* * *

Waking the dead is not easy, or so my mom told me. When 10 A.M. Tuesday morning arrived, I had about four hours of sleep under my belt. Mom tried to rouse me but I don't remember that. She was in a mood when I finally came around. Apparently, I was surly at best, but what did she expect? Four hours of sleep was tough for the living; imagine what it was like for me.

I tried to dress for the mall in something bright and cheerful, but my mood had me searching for something dark and soothing. I settled on a soft gray sweater and jeans. I even added a bright pink tank top under the sweater to perk myself up a bit, but it really wasn't helping. I was tired and grumpy and misery loves company.

After a lot of eye rolling, deep sighing and backtalk, Mom reached her limit.

"Listen, young lady, being Undead is not an excuse for being so negative. I am not spending my day with such an unpleasant person. Shape up or go alone."

I mumbled an apology and shuffled my feet with a little less attitude. I didn't want to shop alone. Besides, Mom had all the money.

We arrived at the mall and went straight to the optical center. I was wearing pink-tinted sunglasses decorated with rhinestones on the rim. I didn't want to take them off and show the clerk my eye color so my mom did all the talking.

"We have her prescription on file and need to pick up a pair of opaque blue contacts."

"Certainly, I'll just get the prescription," the saleswoman said. "Please have a seat over there, where you can try them on to see if they fit comfortably."

"Since Colby's had them fit before, we just need the new

color." Mom leaned closer to the aging saleswoman and added in a whisper, "We're in kind of a hurry. It's that time of the month for her."

I rolled my eyes behind the sunglasses and deliberately turned my back to them. Mom was getting me out of explaining my yellow eyes but still, embarrassing me was hardly my preferred plan of attack.

"Of course." The lady nodded in sympathy, leaving to find my new contacts. She returned with several boxes and asked me which blue I preferred. I picked the one closest to my original eye color, a blue-gray, much to the surprise of my mother. When I had gray eyes, I wanted nothing more than to make them look blue; but now that I had yellow eyes, I wanted nothing more than to look like my original self. Weird, huh?

After our contacts purchase, we hit the cosmetics counter.

I was checking out new colors when the M.A.C. gal, decked out in all black, suggested a sunscreen so I could avoid another sunburn. I stared at her like she was crazy, but Mom gasped when she looked at me under the bright lights of the store. She handed me a mirror. Sure enough, I looked like I had basked on the beaches of Mexico all day. It was sunny outside, but if this was the result of a walk through the parking lot and fluorescent indoor lighting, I had to rethink my desire to be out during the day.

We picked up the highest SPF available from another line and I stocked up on new M.A.C. loose powder and concealer. I even picked up a softer pink blush and lip gloss. I think

Mom's generosity was firmly rooted in pity for my fried skin.

As we window-shopped, I made a mental battle plan to secure my date for Homecoming. I thought of my upcoming Tribunal appointment and briefly wondered if it would be fair to snare Aidan as a date if I couldn't manage to secure a license. It might be pretty traumatic for him to learn his Homecoming date was dead when he arrived to pick me up, corsage in hand.

Shaking off the feelings of uncertainty, I chanted a positive affirmation instead: I was going to get a license and get Aidan as a Homecoming date. Period. End of story.

We left the mall and I could barely keep my eyes open in the car. It was obviously going to be very hard to stay awake during the day. I was beginning to get nervous about going to school again.

Piper showed up at our door right when we arrived home, so I figured she'd been looking out her window, waiting for our return.

I opened the door to her knocking and nodded a greeting. She was lugging a heavy backpack and dropped it unceremoniously on the floor just inside the door.

"Dude, what is up with all the AP classes? Do you always have this much homework?"

She pulled out a paper with my class assignments. I briefly scanned the page and nodded in approval.

"Yep, this is pretty standard." I picked up the bag and was surprised it felt so heavy. Didn't I have superhuman strength now that I was a vampire?

"This is heavy," I said in surprise.

"Yeah, I know. Try lugging it home from school."

"No, I mean this is heavy *for me*. And it shouldn't be. Remember? Last night I was shoving couches through walls, now a book bag is heavy?"

Piper's eyes widened in understanding.

"Oh yeah, that is weird. Maybe you're only strong at night. You know, during prime sucking time?"

I let the sucking comment pass but acknowledged she had a point. Maybe because of my half-blood status, I wasn't always superhuman. Maybe I was only a vampire at night. Sort of like a superhero with a secret identity. I liked the idea of being a mild-mannered cheerleader during the day and a superstrong badass vampire at night.

"I am so tired." I groaned as I half-carried, half-dragged the book bag into the formal living room.

"You can't go to sleep now, or you'll never be able to get up tomorrow. You have to acclimate yourself to being up during the day and sleeping at night."

"Yeah, I guess you're right. So, how was school today?" *Or more importantly, what's everyone saying about me?* I thought.

"Well, everyone was talking about you, of course." She sat down on the bottom stair of the staircase.

"Yeah, did Aidan say anything?"

She looked at me in surprise. "How would I know? It's not like he and I eat lunch together or anything."

She had a good point. Piper and I didn't hang with the same crowd, so she could hardly know what Aidan thought of my disappearance.

"Sorry. Guess I wasn't thinking."

She continued as though I hadn't spoken. "Well, all your teachers were very worried about you and Mrs. Gillman wanted me to double-check if you were still going to make it to your university appointment."

Mrs. Gillman, our school counselor, had secured an interview with one of the board members of Puget Sound University to see which of three applicants would be getting the full-ride scholarship offered this year. I was up against Tim Jones and Pam Lauer. I wasn't too worried about Tim because he didn't have many extracurricular activities, but Pam and I were pretty evenly matched. I wondered briefly if I could use my half-blood status as an affirmative action bonus to get the edge over her.

I shook the thought away and said, "Hey, I got new contacts and makeup. Want to see?"

I went up the stairs to my room, not waiting for an answer. After a short moment, I heard her follow.

I sat down at my vanity and popped the lenses in with practiced ease. I made a little grimace in the mirror. They looked completely fake to me, but much better than the sunglasses alternative.

"What do you think?" I asked.

She stood behind me, looking into the mirror.

"They look okay. Not completely normal, but the best you're going to get, I guess. Hey, wait a minute. I can see your reflection!"

"Well, duh, why wouldn't you?"

"I was doing some research about vampires on the Web and it said you couldn't see a vampire's reflection."

Ah, the wise words of Demonic Angel were coming back to bite me in the butt, yet again.

"Listen, not everything you read about vampires on the Web is true."

"Well of course not, but that fact is also in all the movies. So why wouldn't it be true?"

She made a good point. After all, I thought everything I saw in movies about vampires was true too until I actually became one.

"How come you have a sunburn? Was it that sunny outside today?"

"Oh sure, you believe the reflection thing but don't bat an eyelid about vampires going out during the day. I received this while walking from our car to the mall and maybe the fluorescent lights inside too."

She whistled low. "You're gonna need a pretty strong SPF. What did you get?"

"I picked up a 45 for my face and body. I hope it doesn't clog my pores."

"Look, I have a prescription SPF 60 from my dermatologist. I'll bring that over. It won't clog your pores. Just use the

45 on your body, but maybe you should wear a lot of layers of clothes that cover more skin."

She looked pointedly at my sweater, which had long since slipped off my shoulder to reveal the tank-top strap and a lot of clavicle.

"Fine, I'll cover up more. Thanks for the sunscreen. I'm so glad I have bronzing powder to give me a little color. I hate the pale look." I glanced at Piper, her alabaster skin looking even paler against her jet-black-with-burgundy-undertones hair. "No offense."

She just snorted at me and started pacing around the room like a caged animal. After a couple of minutes playing with my new makeup and watching her pick up, examine and replace half of my things I exploded. "What are you doing?"

"I'm bored, okay? Watching you put on makeup is not my idea of a good time," Piper said.

I was surprised. Rachel, Marci and I could put on makeup and chat about fashion for hours without getting bored.

"What do you want to do?" I asked.

"I don't know, just not this. Have you eaten today?" she asked out of the blue.

"No, I fed last night. Why do you . . . Hey! I get it now. I'm not a token freak show that's going to entertain you with my dark vampire feats, ya know. Is that why you're here? Because now that I'm a nightstalker I'm interesting enough to hang with but when I was just a cheerleader you didn't want to be friends anymore?"

Wow. Where did that *come from?*

"No, that's not why I asked! I just, just . . ." She stumbled over what she wanted to say. "I just didn't want to be your next meal, okay?"

I blinked at her in surprise. Was Piper afraid of me?

"And I never stopped being friends with you because you became a cheerleader. *You* stopped being friends with *me*." Her tone resonated with hurt and resentment. Was I really the one who severed our friendship when I became a cheerleader?

"I'm not going to feed on you, Piper. Not today, not ever. I promise." As for the other issue, I just didn't know where to start.

"It used to be so much easier, when we were little," she said softly.

I thought back to all the times we played games, watched hours of television and entertained ourselves with make-believe. Once we hit middle school, we drifted apart. We didn't hang out during school and stopped running over to each other's house after hours.

"Yeah, I know. But I gotta say, Piper, I'm glad you're here with me now. I mean, I don't know what I would do without someone to talk to about this whole thing."

And I meant it. I don't think Marci and Rachel would ever begin to understand what had happened to me, but Piper seemed to accept me. Even if she was a little freaked out.

"I'm sorry I said I was afraid you were going to feed on me. I know you wouldn't really do that. I guess there's so much about being a vampire I don't know or understand that

I was starting to freak out. I mean, here you are acting like you always do, playing with your makeup and hair, but you aren't supposed to be *you* anymore. You're a vampire. It's just weird you don't act anything like a vampire is supposed to act like, you know?"

"Yeah, tell me about it. Shouldn't I want to wear black and stalk innocent victims and sleep in a coffin and stuff?"

I looked at Piper, seated on my very pink bed with its overhead lace canopy, and we both laughed. I was not a coffin kind of vampire, that was for sure.

We chatted a bit more, and then Piper left for dinner. I eyed my bed longingly. I really wanted a short nap but knew I should fight the urge. I sat down on my bed instead, and then lay down. I told myself I was only going to take a catnap. Just catch a couple of winks.

I awoke suddenly. One look at the clock confirmed my suspicion that I was incapable of catnaps. It was 12 A.M. and I was wide awake. I lay in bed, thinking of my evening out with Thomas, and smiled despite the awkward feeding situation. The way he held me, understanding what I was going through, was so romantic. We were going out again tonight. Well, not a real "date" or anything. Just more of my vampire education, but still, it made me tingly all over.

I decided I would attempt school tomorrow, even if Mom disagreed. Perhaps I could just do a half day and arrive after lunch? Then I could make it to cheer practice. Homecoming was less than a week away and I still hadn't finished learning our dance routine for the pep assembly and halftime show.

Taking a shower felt wonderful, but all of the scented products had to go. My super-sniffer wasn't up to the task anymore.

Wearing a big fluffy pink robe, I walked around my room to gather up pedicure equipment. It was time to update my toe color. I glanced out the window: Standing in my driveway was Charles Winthrop. Boy, that guy did not take no for an answer.

Throwing on jeans and a sweatshirt, I hurried downstairs to confront my attacker, again.

"What are you doing here?" I demanded, shivering in the cold evening breeze.

"Didn't your mother ever tell you that you'll catch your death going out with wet hair?" He tipped his head to one side as he spoke.

"Ha, ha. Look, I told you I am not going to live with you. Why don't we try something new, like you stopping by only when I call you? What a novel idea. Why are you here?" I repeated.

"I come bearing sad news," he replied, looking anything but sad.

"What kind of sad news?" I asked slowly, my mind racing with all sorts of implications. Where was Piper, Aunt Chloe and my folks?

"I'm afraid she didn't take it well."

"Who are you talking about?"

"Why, Jill, of course. She was part of our family but no more. See, my dear? See why it is so important that you come live with me? Only I can protect you. She didn't come with

me either and now look what happened." He looked heaven-
ward and begged an answer from the sky: "Why must all of
my children be taken from me?"

"I have no idea what you're talking about, Chuck, but I
meant what I said—stay away from me." I turned to go back
into the house.

"Colby, it is a Tribunal Investigator's job to carry out the
Princes' orders. Remember that." He pressed a card into my
hand and stepped back.

I ignored the card and looked at him, trying to gauge what
he was telling me. Chuck just smiled pleasantly, as though we
were discussing the weather. What a nutter.

I went back inside and locked the door behind me. Chuck
had given me a card with a phone number on it. Maybe he
was taking me seriously. I snorted. Who was I kidding, and
who was Jill? Why was she taken away? Thomas was an Investigator and I didn't doubt Chuck was trying to freak me
out about something.

Instead of wasting too many brain cells thinking about
Chuck's demented musings, I took my time getting ready for
meeting Thomas. It wasn't a date or anything, but I did
want to look good. Being Undead was no excuse for looking
like a slob.

As I painted my toenails, I tried to ignore the little voice in
my head that said even if Chuck was nuts, why would he
make up a weird story? He knew I wasn't frightened of him,
so why try to scare me with some story of a girl who didn't
want his protection?

I checked the clock one last time, made sure my toes were dry and hurried to change my clothes. I wore my contacts instead of sunglasses and the reflection in the mirror confirmed my suspicions that I looked like a normal teenager. And a rather hip one at that.

I met Thomas at the door wearing boots, a miniskirt and poncho. I added the newsboy cap at the last minute because I felt it had a 1940s look that Thomas might appreciate. He smiled when he saw me.

"Where to this time?" I asked, after sliding into the Camaro.

"I thought you might want to check out the library."

Surely my ears were deceiving me.

"The library? Isn't that closed?"

He winked at me and revved the engine. "Not the library I have in mind."

I smiled halfheartedly, mentally kicking myself for reading more into our "date" than there was. When Thomas said he wanted to help me with my Tribunal case, he meant it literally. It obviously wasn't a come-on, like a "let's study together" where you meet and then end up making out.

We drove south until we reached the Burien area, then headed west, until we reached the Puget Sound. The moon was hovering over the water and the scene was breathtaking. He parked his car in the driveway of an old home with a waterfront view and escorted me to the door.

"Where's the library?" I asked.

"This is a vampire safe house that also contains a library. The Tribunal owns it."

I counted the other cars in the driveway—five—and let out a discouraged breath. We had little chance of being alone.

The entryway of the home offered a choice of stairs going up or down; we went down to a huge room lined with bookshelves, chock-full of books. It really was a library. Crap.

Several people were reading at one of the conference tables. Another table held several very old-looking volumes. Thomas led me there.

"I took the liberty of picking these out for you to look through. I think they will give you the best understanding of the culture." He pulled the top book off the stack and plopped it down in front of me. Dust arose when he opened it and I coughed a bit as he flipped the pages.

A stern-looking woman with bifocal glasses that slipped to the end of her nose shushed me from behind an ancient desk.

Thomas ignored the warning and said, "Start here and read until the end of the chapter. I will mark the other books so you know which chapters to read."

I sat at the table, mouth agape as he pulled the stack in front of him and began flagging passages with Post-it notes. He worked quickly, obviously knowing which material each book contained. When he was done, I was barely a page through my first reading.

"There you go. I will be back in a couple of hours to see how you are doing."

"You're leaving me?!"

"You can cover the material faster without me here. That way you won't be tempted to stop and ask questions that might be covered in another book. We will review the material together when I return. Good luck."

He waved and took the steps two at a time. I didn't even have time to admire his layered fashions or inhale his delicious cookie scent.

I let out a disgruntled sigh and turned back to my reading. At least I could do this. Studying was second nature to me, but after an hour of reviewing the driest text ever put on paper, my eyes were aching. Even though I didn't see the point of reading about the entire Tribunal legislature, history and such, I had to admit some of it was interesting.

I was particularly fascinated with the passages that talked about rogue vampires and half-blood creation, but since all of those stories ended in eliminating the half-bloods and torturing the rogue vampire to death, they didn't leave me with a warm and fuzzy feeling for my fellow vampires.

As a matter of fact, I felt it was downright unfair to punish the half-blood for the mistakes of its Creator. It reminded me of ancient times, when the sins of the father were passed down to the children for many generations. People and civilization had evolved; why couldn't the vampire world?

I decided to photocopy some legislation of interest and approached the librarian who had shushed me.

"Excuse me," I took pains to whisper, "where can I make some copies?"

"No," she said, not even looking up from her task of stamping books.

Huh? "I'm sorry, I don't think you heard me correctly. I was asking for a copy machine?"

"I heard you correctly and the answer is no. Half-bloods are not allowed to copy vampire legislature."

I tapped my toe impatiently. Bigotry aside, if I was allowed to review the legislature, why wasn't I allowed to copy it?

I turned around and slowly walked back to my pile of books, noticing several faces smirk in my direction. Not one sympathetic vampire among them and they all practically reeked of superiority.

Oh, I don't think so. This may be a vampire library but it's still America. I watched another vampire come out of a door behind the librarian's desk, his hands full of copies. So there it was.

Standing up with my book, I walked toward the librarian again, this time ignoring her completely and walking around her desk to the door.

"What do you think you're doing?" she shrieked at me.

"Shhhh," I chided. "You're in a library. Kindly use your indoor voice."

"I told you that you can't make any copies." She stood up and both of us reached the door at the same time.

"Listen, lady, I've got all night and all *day* to wait to make copies. Can you say the same?"

We stared at each other and she finally backed down with an exasperated sniff. We both knew Thomas would make any copies I needed the minute he came back anyway, so the standoff was a moot point at best. She'd done it to prove something to me.

*   *   *

When Thomas returned, I had skimmed much of his material and was researching other items I thought were more relevant.

"Are you ready for a break?" he asked, handing me a bottled water.

I stood up and stretched my back, taking satisfaction in the way his gaze went to my bare belly when my poncho rode up. *Hah! Take me to a library and leave me when I thought we were on a date. Serves you right,* I thought smugly.

We took a walk upstairs and I was surprised to find a comfortably outfitted living room and a deck running along the entire floor.

"I bet the sunset on the water is amazing," I said to Thomas as he offered me a seat on the deck.

"I wouldn't know." He smirked in my direction and took a drink of his water.

Duh! I wasn't very good at thinking before I spoke around him. "Sorry, I forgot," I offered lamely.

Thomas sat next to me and patted my knee in forgiveness. The gesture was almost brotherly. What was with me lately? I couldn't get Aidan to commit to a simple date and now I couldn't get Thomas to look at me as anything other than a genetic mutant. It seemed like the only person who wanted to be with me was that fruitcake Winthrop and I wasn't that desperate yet—was I?

I leaned forward abruptly. "Well, it's getting late and I don't want to keep you out past your vampire time. Thanks for the library information." I stood up, plainly ready to leave.

Thomas said, "What's your hurry? Tell me what you learned today."

I very much wanted to whack him upside the head with one of those big dusty books. "I'm not the one who'll be incinerated when the sun comes up."

He glanced at my face in surprise. I could have *tried* to keep the hostility out of my voice. He stood up and asked, "Are you mad at me for something?"

I fidgeted a moment, shifting my weight from one foot to the other. "No, no. What reason could I possibly have to be mad at you?"

His eyebrows rose in response. I really, *really* needed to learn how to disguise the hostility in my voice.

"Colby, I want you to do well with the Tribunal, but I can't do the research for you."

I gaped at him. He thought I was mad because I had to do my own work?

"I don't need you to do my work for me, Thomas. I'll have you know I can and did research circles around you—I found more information on my behalf *by myself* than in those passages you outlined for me."

"Then what's the matter with you?" he exploded, clearly not understanding anything.

"Oh, you're such a—such a—bloodsucking *man*!" I turned to stomp away, but Thomas was faster and whipped me around to face him.

"I don't get you, Colby! You are so independent and yet so vulnerable that I'm just not sure how to treat you. You know how important this summons is, yet when I try to help you, you get mad at me."

When he put it that way, I did sound a tad unreasonable. It was just that I had such expectations about our evening together; spending it alone in a dusty library with a bunch of hostile vampires was not one of them.

"I just didn't expect to spend my night out with you all alone with a bunch of old books, that's all," I mumbled into my shoulder.

It took Thomas a moment to realize what I was saying, but his vampire hearing was very good, so there was no pretending I'd said something different. He leaned forward, taking my face in his hands, and looked into my eyes.

"Our time together is precious and short, Colby. I can't even think about how I really want to spend it if I am going to save you."

I felt a surge of warmth start in the pit of my stomach and flow through my limbs. He did like me.

"Oh, okay then." I sounded so lame!

He dropped his hands and ushered me back into the library. We gathered our stuff and left in his car, both of us quiet and lost in our own thoughts.

We made it back to my house in record time. "Thanks for

taking me to the library," I offered when the silence started to get awkward.

"I'm glad to be of service," he countered neutrally.

Nodding, I blew out a breath and said, "Well, I guess I'll see you later. I'm going to try to go back to school tomorrow."

"Are you sure that's wise?" Thomas questioned.

"I have a college scholarship interview Thursday night I just can't miss. Also, I don't know the dance routine for Homecoming. I can't stop going to school indefinitely."

Thomas nodded briskly, his lips tightening in disapproval.

"See ya," I said, equally cool, and opened the car door.

"Colby?" Thomas surprised me by saying.

Somewhat annoyed, I turned back to him. "What?"

Before I could register a thought, his lips were on mine.

Nine

Despite our very low body temperature, I can assure you that vampire lips—or Thomas's, at least—are warm, soft and oh so perfect. He held me close with his hand on the back of my neck and was so *confident* with his kisses that it left no doubt in my mind he knew what he was doing.

He deepened the kiss and just when I thought we were going to settle in for a nice long lip-lock session, he pulled away and said, "I'll see you tomorrow night at the Krispy Kreme, okay?"

Dazed, I mumbled, "Sure," and slid out of the car, floating all the way to the front door. I dreamily stepped into the house and hummed down the corridor to the kitchen. Still singing to myself, I dumped my research next to the kitchen computer and twirled each bar stool around, as though I were dancing with them. Yes, excellent blackmail material if anyone happened to be filming me at this hour, but I didn't care.

I had been thoroughly kissed by a very dreamy vampire and that was all that mattered. A thought occurred to me as I twirled and abruptly stopped my daydreaming. What if Thomas didn't get home before sunrise? I checked the clock. It was almost 6 A.M. I swung myself in front of the computer to pull up a local news site. They always listed sunrise and sunset times.

In my frenzy, I completely ignored the headlines and breathed a sigh of relief when I saw 6:45 as the listed sunrise.

I went to bed but sleep eluded me. I was restless. Every sound, every scent invaded my head. It was like being superwired on caffeine and told to keep still. Suddenly it was 11 A.M. After Thomas's kiss, I felt I could take on the world, so I decided to try school for a half a day.

My blue contacts were in, self-tanner had been slathered liberally over my pale skin and I was dressed in my favorite sweater and jeans. Mom generously applied the SPF to any skin that was left uncovered. I was almost normal, except I was very crabby. I like my sleep and when I don't get enough I can be very snippy, as my mother was quick to remind me when I sarcastically answered her homework question.

"I've about had it with your attitude, missy. If you want to attend school with your friends, you're going to have to get used to sleeping in four-hour increments. Otherwise, you can finish school at night and get your GED," she told me.

"Never! I will *not* get a GED. I am going to graduate at the top of my class like I planned and you can't stop me."

"Undead or not, Colby, I am your mother and you will do as you're told. Now gather your books and get in the car. I'm going to be late showing the Valentine house if we don't leave right now. I don't know why you insisted on going back to school today, anyway. We haven't even filed a police report yet!"

I flounced into the kitchen to get my book bag. Mom could be such a pain sometimes.

When we reached school, I kissed her good-bye. She sniffed a bit at the gesture. It was the closest thing she was going to get to an "I'm sorry" and we both knew it. The bell rang for fourth period to start so I hurried through the front doors of the school and headed for the office. I checked in and everyone wished me well and hugged me. It was nice to be so coddled by the secretaries. My school counselor came out of her office to remind me about the PSU interview tomorrow night and I assured her I was up for it.

As far as I was concerned, it was business as usual but everyone else wanted to talk about what happened and try to get any new dirt on the situation. By sixth period, my already strained good humor was almost at its breaking point.

The person I really wanted to talk to was Aidan. I was holding out little hope of being his Homecoming date, since rumor had it he was taking Allison, but I wanted to see where we stood. Sure, I was still thinking about Thomas's kiss, but I wanted to line up my options. Aidan was at his locker when I finally tracked him down at the end of the day.

"Hey, Aidan. How are you?"

He turned quickly and I was disappointed to see surprise and unease wash over his handsome face.

"Hi," he said, obviously trying to get all of the stuff he needed out of his locker in an attempt to escape me as soon as possible.

"I was kinda hoping we could go somewhere and talk." Sure, I was making the first move but I had to. Aidan was probably still too spooked by my attack to ask me out again.

"Uh, I don't think I can," he replied, looking around desperately for someone to run interference.

"Oh, okay. I just thought since we were supposed to go out before I was attacked that we could try to get together now." Did I mention I spent no time playing coy when I was tired and cranky?

"Yeah, I don't think so. Listen, Colby, do you know I spent hours with the police because everyone said I was taking you home on Friday? They thought I *killed* you or something and if wasn't for Allison confirming I was with her, they would have put me in jail!"

I winced at his tone. He was pretty mad. I guess I couldn't blame him. I had told anyone who would listen that he was taking me home. It hadn't occurred to me that the police would think of him as a prime suspect.

"Oh, I'm so sorry, Aidan! I had no idea. I just thought after we spoke about hooking up after the game Friday, that you would, you know, drive me home."

"Yeah, well, I gotta go." And Aidan Reynolds, star football player and my imaginary Homecoming date, pushed past me down the hall. In front of everybody, I might add.

Diva Raine, who so obviously had been listening to our private conversation, decided to give her two cents' worth.

"Oh, too bad, Cheesy. Looks like you're not all that lucky lately."

"Step off, Rebecca. I'm warning you." I was in no mood for her dramatic cattiness.

"Really? You're warning me? Or you'll what? Tell everyone you were with me and then fake another attack?" Her two lemmings snickered.

"What are you talking about? I didn't fake any attack."

"Yeah, that's not what I heard. Everyone's talking about it. Your pitiful attempt to get Aidan to notice you by claiming you fell down the hill after the Eastside Attacker startled you." She shook her head at me. "Please, Cheesy, no one's buying your little helpless act. Next time try filing a police report to make it look more realistic."

She swept down the hall, leaving me with my mouth hanging open. *Did everyone think I faked my attack? Is that what Aidan thought? Who would say such a thing about me?*

Then Allison passed by and the smirk on her face told me everything I needed to know. Her father was a police officer. Sure, I couldn't *prove* she was the one who started the rumor, but I would lay even money and my Tommy Hilfiger denim jacket that she was responsible for leaking information about my not-yet-filed police report. I was so angry, I didn't know what to do. But if Allison hoped she could bring me to tears, she was sadly mistaken. I tended to get mad where others would cry. Like those people who laughed during funerals, my emotions were hard-wired weird.

Taking a deep breath, I turned around and started walking down the hall. The whispering was all over: the debates over my faking an attack, what people thought of me in general and whether I would land Homecoming Queen now. Keeping my head up, I pretended I didn't hear a thing. It was time for cheerleading practice and I wasn't about to give these people the satisfaction of seeing me break down. No matter how badly I wanted to scream and kick something.

I went straight to the girls' locker room and changed. I was just about to join the rest of my squad when Mrs. Frost intercepted me.

"Colby, dear, how are you feeling?"

"I'm okay, Mrs. Frost. Just getting ready to head to practice."

"Yes, that's why I'm here."

Slowing down, I zipped up my backpack and shut my locker.

"Dear, we didn't really know when to expect you back, so the squad changed the routine accordingly and . . . well . . . we took you out."

"So what are you saying?"

"I'm guess I'm saying you won't be able to perform with the squad at the assembly or at the game," she said.

"But I'm the cheer squad captain!" I was stunned.

"Well, yes, but Allison stepped up when you were attacked. She feels that it would not be fair for the squad to have to learn new positions with so little time left before the performance, and I tend to agree. You can still cheer at the game, of course."

"So you're saying I'm no longer captain?"

"Of course not!" she protested. "You can resume your duties after the Homecoming game. We really didn't expect you back so soon, dear."

"And who told you that?"

"Why, Allison did. She was more surprised than any of us when you came back to school. She thinks you may have returned too soon. She's very worried about you."

Yeah, I just bet she is.

Mrs. Frost left me alone and I reviewed my first day back at school. Aidan hated me, I was demoted on the cheer squad and would not be able to perform the halftime routine and everyone thought I faked my attack. Oh yeah, and I was still Undead without a license. Could today get any worse?

I skipped practice. I was so mad at Allison I worried I would do something to give myself away, like suck her dry. The thought made me smile. I went home instead, hoping to get a nap in before I tackled my homework and prepped for my interview.

I walked home (no longer concerned about being attacked) and crawled into bed. Several hours later I awoke to the sound of clanging in the kitchen. I investigated the noise to find Great-Aunt Chloe trying to find the muffin tins.

"Where in the world does your mother keep those darn things? I swear this kitchen has no rhyme or reason to it," she grumbled.

I bent down and pulled them out of the drawer under the double oven. I handed them to her with raised eyebrows.

"Well, heavens, that's a stupid place for a drawer."

Moving toward the kitchen table, I let Aunt Chloe continue her grumbling when I saw the paper. One headline caught my attention:

LOCAL GIRL DIES IN FREAK ACCIDENT
ONE WEEK AFTER SURVIVING ATTACK

I sat down and read the article, hardly believing what was in black and white in front of me. Jill Schneider, the local teen who'd escaped the clutches of the Eastside Attacker just two weeks ago, fell out of a tree house and impaled herself on a branch.

This was what Chuck meant last night. Impaling yourself on a tree branch certainly fell under the category of "freak accident" but I wasn't buying it for a minute. Had Thomas done this? Could the guy who showed me how to feed and comforted me so sweetly kill Jill Schneider because she was a half-blood? Had he shown her all the vampire hot spots, told her cute anecdotal stories about his youth and kissed her under the full moon, all the while plotting to kill her?

Ten

I raced to the kitchen computer and looked up the Schneiders on 411.com. There were many listed but only one family on the Plateau. I got the address and plugged it into Mapquest. They lived just at the bottom of the hill. Then I grabbed the paper and ran over to Piper's house, ignoring my aunt's queries.

If Piper was surprised to see me, she didn't show it. She looked at me like she always did, sort of a blank look of recognition and tepid friendliness. Piper wasn't known for her spontaneous displays of emotion.

"Hey," she said and stepped back from the door to let me in.

"Hey." I gave her the newspaper and stepped into the house. My mother accuses teenagers of killing the English language because we use so few words, but what Mom didn't get was the volume of communication we put into each word. For instance, what Piper was really saying was, "It's good to see you up and around. You're looking pretty normal and are welcome to come in my house because even though I know you're a vampire, I am not afraid of you and to prove it you may enter."

And my response meant, "I'm glad you aren't afraid of me and that you care if I am okay. I'm here because I need your help and you letting me in shows you are up to helping me." So now you know the truth about monosyllabic teenage communication.

I followed her past the living room where her parents were enjoying the evening news. Neither looked up when I entered so I didn't offer a greeting. Once we were alone in the kitchen Piper asked, "What's this?"

"Did you read about Jill Schneider? The other girl who was attacked?"

Piper looked down at the paper and blew out a sigh. Then she looked me in the eye and nodded.

"Coincidence?" I asked.

Piper snorted in response.

"Yeah, that's what I thought."

I looked at the plate of cookies sitting on her kitchen island with longing. Chocolate chip and walnuts.

"What's the plan?" she asked me.

I picked up one of the cookies and smelled it appreciatively. "I was thinking about stopping by her house to offer my condolences to her parents. Try to get a feel for the situation."

Piper took the cookie from me with a stern look. "Don't even think about it. If you hurl on the hardwood, Mom will have a fit. Come on." She started to put the cookie back but changed her mind and took a bite. She had a way of kicking a person when she was down. Then she grabbed a set of keys hanging by the door that led to the garage.

"You don't have to do this, you know."

She looked at me with the half-eaten cookie clutched between her teeth and rolled her eyes. Okay, she was in all the way. That was all I needed to know.

After she finished the cookie she called out to the living room, "Mom, I'm going to the mall with Colby. Be back in awhile."

"With who?" her mother called back.

"Colby. You know, from next door? She wants my advice on her homecoming dress." I looked at Piper in horror and she winked at me.

"Oh, all right dear. Have fun," her mother replied.

"What? No questions about my attack or anything?" I asked, surprised her mom didn't give me the third degree.

"Cold medicine. Mom's fighting a cold and has a huge presentation tomorrow. The NyQuil wipes her out. Dad was probably sleeping," Piper explained.

We entered the garage and hopped into a black Honda Accord. We pulled out of the driveway and she said, "We don't know where we're going."

"Actually, I do. I looked up directions to their house on Mapquest after I read the article."

We took several winding turns but, as the crow flies, Jill didn't live that far from us. She went to Newport, but there were two high schools on the Plateau and another two in the area.

We pulled into a "nice" cul-de-sac, where all the "nice" houses formed a perfectly "nice" suburban community. A lot of teenagers on the Eastside were from upper middle-class families, thanks to the booming computer industry. Each house was decorated for Halloween with pumpkins, hay and gourds. All the houses save one—the Schneider house.

We sat in the car, neither of us anxious to bombard a mourning family with probing questions about Tribunals and vampire investigators.

"I kind of thought this would be easier," I said to Piper, still unwilling to unbuckle my seat belt.

"Yeah," she agreed, but at least she opened her door. I could hardly remain in the car, cowardly cringing, while Piper courageously carried out our plan so I rushed to join her.

"Let me do the talking," I said once I caught up.

We knocked at the door and a very motherly looking lady opened it. She was older than we expected. I thought she might be Jill's grandma.

"Mrs. Schneider?" I asked uncertainly.

The woman nodded to us. She was wearing an apron and her short gray hair was perfectly curled in tight waves.

"We knew Jill from swim team. We always competed

against each other and liked her a lot. We just wanted to stop by and let you know how sorry we are about what happened," I said.

Mrs. Schneider nodded again and stood aside, ushering us in, as her eyes misted over.

I was immediately struck by how stark the home was. There were no pictures of Jill anywhere. The paper said Jill was an athlete involved in track and swimming, and was also on the dance team. There are twenty-three pictures of me in various stages of my school career in my living room alone. Where were the pictures of Jill?

We perched ourselves in the formal living room on a suitably uncomfortable couch while Mrs. Schneider sat opposite of us in a very rigid wingback chair.

"So you girls knew Jill?" she asked politely. Both Piper and I noticed the lack of refreshments offered and took it as a sign to get to the point as quickly as we dared.

"Yes, we did. We were all shocked when she was attacked but then the accident. . . ." I trailed off, hoping she would step in and provide some more details.

"Yes, we were quite devastated."

It was the appropriate response but the sheer lack of feeling behind the statement made my skin crawl. Was Mrs. Schneider medicated to keep her calm or was it something else? Something was not right in the Schneider household.

Piper surprised me by stepping in. "We understand this must be a very difficult time for you, ma'am, and the last thing we want to do is cause you more pain."

Mrs. Schneider studied Piper for a moment and I couldn't help but wonder if Jill's regular friends had piercings. She finally replied, "There are all sorts of pain. Death seems like a release sometimes."

Piper and I looked at each other with raised brows and then back at Mrs. Schneider. She was looking over Piper's ear at something on the sofa table behind us.

Curious, I stood up to pace the room, but I was really trying to angle toward the table. There was some sort of paperwork scattered about. Piper asked how Mrs. Schneider was holding up as I maneuvered my way closer. I couldn't read anything but I recognized the crest of the Tribunal on the stationery immediately.

Mrs. Schneider trailed off in mid-conversation, staring into space. Piper looked over her shoulder at me and mouthed, "Weird." I walked back to the vacant-looking woman and asked, "Did Jill say anything about the night she was attacked, anything other than what she told the police?"

I might as well have slapped Mrs. Schneider for the reaction my comment caused. The once coolly detached woman started blathering incoherently, clutching her hands to her chest in fear.

"They promised they would leave us alone. They promised! Why are you here? Who are you? They said we would be safe!"

Piper jumped to her feet and I moved around the couch, reaching toward Mrs. Schneider to reassure her we meant no harm, but she slapped at my hands and accidentally knocked my sunglasses askew. When she looked in my eyes she shrieked and dove behind her chair.

"Leave us alone, we did our part! Jill is gone, isn't that enough? We haven't told anyone. She was a good girl, she never hurt anyone. We never hurt anyone. Just leave us alone!"

Footsteps pounded on the floor above us as if someone was rushing to Mrs. Schneider's aid. Piper and I did the only thing we could do in the face of such hysteria and a possible tussle. We ran like hell to the car and sped away.

Once we were a couple blocks from poor Mrs. Schneider and my heart had stopped leaping out of my throat I said, "I'm guessing Jill didn't die in a freak accident."

"Ya think?" Piper retorted sarcastically.

"Did you see that poor woman?" I continued, ignoring her comment. "I've never seen anyone lose it like that. I mean, she was *scared*. And they didn't have any pictures of Jill anywhere. It was like she never existed."

I shivered at the thought of my parents wiping away all visible signs of my existence if the Tribunal decided not to give me a license. I didn't like the way my thoughts were going. Piper said what I couldn't bring myself to.

"Colby, do you think you have a chance with the Tribunal?"

I stared straight ahead, ignoring the orange lights and decorative witches "crashed" into every other door on the block.

I raked my fingers through my hair and whispered, "I'm so screwed."

For once Piper didn't offer a sarcastic quip. She just nodded sagely in agreement.

Eleven

Waiting at the Krispy Kreme for Thomas seemed to take a lifetime. When he finally sat down with tea in hand, I wasted no time with pleasantries.

"Tell me about Jill Schneider, Thomas."

His eyes widened a moment and he paused before taking a sip of his tea. "There is nothing to tell," he replied.

"Eent. Wrong answer. Try again."

"It is none of your concern, Colby."

"Eent. Wrong again. Boy, you really suck at this. It's very much my business when I find out there was another vampire like me who was eliminated. You should have told me. I have a right to know."

"It is not my job to inform you about every turned mongrel out there. And you have no rights. Not yet, anyway."

"Not your job to inform me?" I asked incredulously. Man, this guy was something else! "It was you, wasn't it? You eliminated Jill."

"I am an Investigator for the Tribunal. I am not at liberty to discuss other cases."

"But she was like me!" I cried out.

"No! She was not like you!" He slammed his hand down on the table, causing everyone in the booths around us to stare. He lowered his voice and continued.

"She was never like you. She was indecisive, weak and incapable of sound decisions."

"She was only fifteen!" I said in her defense. What an insensitive jerk.

"Yes, she was fifteen. Another strike against her. She did not possess your maturity and strength. Even with those attributes, I'm still fearful what the Tribunal will decide for you."

I stared into his hypnotic green eyes, unaffected by the mesmerizing power contained there. I was immune to his vampire voodoo but I wanted to have his undivided attention for what I was about to say.

"Listen to me, you bloodsucking bigot. Your kind created 'mongrels' like Jill and me. You have a responsibility toward us. You don't get to sweep it all under the carpet because you can't control your full-bloods."

Thomas sighed deeply. "Colby, you don't understand. We are talking about an ancient species here who can't accept change. Most of the elders are"—he struggled for the right words—"a bit touched in the head. They don't act reasonably

or think rationally. They have lived most of their lives in fear
of being murdered. Our laws and government evolved to protect all vampires and keep our lines pure. They don't want a
bunch of mongrels out there causing problems."

"Like I just said—a bunch of bigots." I took a deep breath
and continued to look him in the eye. "I don't have a chance,
do I, Thomas? They aren't going to listen to me at all, are
they?"

He stared back unflinchingly. "Things don't look good,
Colby."

"Oh." I couldn't think of anything else to say. I wasn't going to get a chance to defend myself after all. I was up against
thousands of years of fear, bigotry and—if I understood
Thomas correctly—ancient, whacked-out vampires.

"What if I knew where my Creator was? What if I turned
him in? Would that prove my worthiness? I mean, it worked
for you." It was a shot in the dark, but worth a try.

Thomas weighed his words carefully. "If your Creator was
returned to us, it would mean his death. He wouldn't come
willingly. It might exonerate you or you might be killed
alongside him. It is up to the elders. They are"—he paused
again—"unpredictable."

My mind raced at the thought of getting back at the one
who'd gotten me into this mess. If it wasn't for him, I would
be at cheerleading practice, leading a normal life. He de-
served to get staked for attacking and changing a teenage
girl, dooming her to an eternity of adolescent hormones and
breakouts.

"I don't like the look on your face," Thomas said, interrupting my thoughts.

"Really? Well, I don't like the thought of getting staked before being named Homecoming Queen, so we all have some adjusting to do, don't we?"

"Colby . . ." His voice was low and forbidding.

"What did you expect, Thomas? That I would be thrilled with the news and gratefully follow you back to these elders like a sheep to the slaughter? Uh, I don't think so. What do I have to lose? I either get killed by Chuck or one of your vampire police."

"Charles Winthrop is very elusive. I have been tracking him for the last six months and have come up with nothing. Finding him is a lost cause for you."

"Oh, is that so? Because you can't find him no one can, huh? I got news for you, buster—I've seen him not once, but twice since he changed me. So if little ol' mutant me can find him where big bad Terminator vampire can't get a clue then maybe you need to find a new line of work." I flounced back into my seat.

Thomas blinked at my outburst several times before replying, "You have seen him twice and said nothing to me?"

"Yeah, I guess we both have our dirty little secrets," I retorted, my voice dripping with sarcasm. *He doesn't tell me about Jill and now he has the nerve to look hurt that I didn't tell him about Chuck? I don't think so.*

"Colby, this is an impossible situation. I can see you're distressed . . ."

"Hah!"

"But you have to be realistic. Learning about the vampire way so you can defend yourself to the Tribunal is your only hope now. Not chasing down a rogue vampire you can't possibly outwit."

He was using his soothing-an-unreasonable-child voice and just to add insult to injury, he thought I was too stupid to live if I chose to use my time finding Winthrop. I couldn't believe I kissed him, and liked it. A lot.

I stood up and calmly wrapped the pink chenille scarf my aunt had knitted for me around my neck. I picked up my gloves and pulled them on, tucking each finger in with flair. I grabbed my purse and looked down at him, trying to ignore how great he looked in his worn cotton pullover.

"I am going after Chuck. Stay out of my way. I may not be Blooded, Thomas, but I am something you're not. *Desperate*."

I meant to sweep from the room in a dramatic exit, but Thomas grabbed my wrist.

"I still want to help you defend yourself to the Tribunal."

I used my vampire strength to pry his fingers off me and replied, "The trouble is, Thomas, I don't trust you anymore. If the Tribunal decides I don't get a license, then they send you to do the dirty work. So I have to ask myself: why would you want to help me when you're only going to kill me in the end?"

He acted as though I had slapped him. "I wish you no harm, Colby, I thought you knew that. But understand this: there are many ways to die and if the elders decide that is your fate, I would make sure it was painless for you."

I was so shocked to hear this revelation that I sat back down. "Would you really be my executioner, Thomas?" I asked incredulously. Who did this guy think he was, anyway?

Thomas looked past my shoulder. "It is one of my duties for the Vampire Council."

I gaped at him, for once in my life speechless. I'd thought we were starting to become friends—more than friends, actually. I confided in him about what it was like to be different, a mutant freak in a world of full-blooded vampires, and he sat there supposedly comforting me when all the while he was responsible for the deaths of how many half-bloods before me? Maybe even Jill.

"You *are* the half-blood executioner," I whispered accusingly and felt a small satisfaction when he winced.

"I am not the only one but I requested the duty, in case things didn't turn out well for you."

I couldn't believe my ears. He wanted to kill me? No, he not only wanted to kill me, he asked to kill me!

"You *requested* it?! What about Jill, Thomas? Did you promise to help her, get all cozy and then throw her out a tree?"

His head snapped back. "Jill Schneider's case is none of your concern and will only distract you from what you need to do. Right now the only thing that matters is making a strong defense to get your license."

I felt my lower lip quiver and bit it to stop the tremble. I was not going to cry in front of him. "The only thing that matters to me, right now, is getting as far away from you as I can."

I raced out of the doughnut shop and made it to my car before Thomas grabbed my upper arm.

"Let go!" I screeched like an outraged parrot. And adding to my distinguished role of a woman scorned, I stomped my feet like a two-year-old. "Let go! Let go! Let go!" Stomp, stomp, stomp.

Thomas stepped back, putting distance between himself and the shrieking toddler I'd become, and, with a last unfathomable look, spun on his heel and left.

After he was gone I started to shake. Sure I talked big but I was scared. I was only sixteen! I was fighting for my survival. I was all alone and the one person I thought understood me was going to wait to kill me as painlessly as possible.

"Nicely done."

Winthrop was standing on the passenger side of my car.

I jumped a bit, even though I tried to pretend I hadn't. I couldn't help it, my nerves were shot.

"Do you see why you should be with me now? We are the same, you and I," he stated flatly, his brown eyes looking very deep and pensive.

"Really? The same? Hmmm, I can't remember the last time I attacked a helpless girl, changed her into the walking Undead and threw her in a ravine." I tapped my chin thoughtfully. "Hmmm. Where is my memory?"

He smiled, showing his bloodstained fangs and teeth. He was freshly fed, it seemed. "There is strength in numbers. I could protect you."

I hated to admit it, but it was a tempting offer. Thomas

was offering a pain-free execution, while Winthrop was offering me a chance to live. I doubted ol' Chuck could really keep me safe, although he had supposedly managed to elude Thomas for almost six months.

"You've helped me enough, thanks." I wondered if I could truss him up and take him back to the Tribunal with me.

"The Tribunal will never let you live." He stopped smiling when he announced that verdict.

"How can you be so sure they haven't already given me a license?" I asked him.

He laughed at me. "The Dark Ones wear their licenses with pride." He had me there. I was ring-free at the moment.

"Why do you think they'll never give me a license? I think I'll take my chances. I can be pretty charming when I want to."

My retort caused instant fury to cross his features. "A half-blood will never be allowed to live in vampire society. Never! You are a fool."

"Then enlighten me. You're a vampire—explain why you can't let half-bloods into your society."

His eyes narrowed, looking for the insult he was sure I'd slipped in there. I suppose he was pretty pleased to realize my interest was actually genuine because his features returned to the usual carefully schooled polite mask. What a whack job!

"There was a time before vampires were reduced to bureaucrats pushing papers and filing 'Blood Wars' when our people were strong. I have been told all my existence that half-bloods will never be accepted and that is *not* going to change for you." He wrinkled his nose in derision. Now I was starting to get angry. He was the one who created me and damned me to start with.

"Listen, *Chuck,* you are the reason I'm in this mess in the first place. Why should I come with you? You're living on the edge, barely a step ahead of the Investigators. You don't seem to be offering a whole lot of security, in my opinion. And you look like a transient who lives under the bypass"—I nodded scornfully at his fraying coat and fingerless gloves—"so why should I believe you could protect me at all?"

He cocked his head at me, like a curious bird, and in the blink of an eye, he was beside me. I stood perfectly still while he pushed some strands of hair away from my ear and whispered, "Because I'm still here, aren't I?"

I turned my head and our gazes locked. There was something stirringly familiar about his eyes. As though I knew him or should know something about him. I felt a magnetic pull that beckoned me closer, to give in and trust him. Thomas had warned me I might feel this way about my Creator and I had scoffed at the idea. Now I could see what he was talking about.

As distasteful as it sounded, to get my license I needed to bring Chuck in. And doing that meant I would have to suck up to him. Ewwww.

"I'm not sure. I have to think. Will you—will you meet me tomorrow night?" I whispered uncertainly, playing the part of reluctant Undead.

He smiled in delight at my apparent change of heart and leaned forward to put a brotherly kiss on my forehead. Gag. It took all my strength not to squirm or pull away. If I was going to get my license, I was going to need Chuck; but still, putting up with his affection was almost more than I could bear.

In an instant he was gone, a quick blur through the parking lot and into the night.

I got into my car and drove home. It was close to midnight and I was wide awake. It was a school night but I knew I would never be able to sleep. Funny thing, I didn't feel like going out and wandering the streets either. Being a vampire should be more exciting, but I was more of a veg-on-the-couch and watch movies kind of gal.

As I went by Piper's house I was glad to see a light in her window still burning. I parked, then, picking up some pebbles, walked into her side lawn and threw them in the direction of her room. After a moment, she looked out in confusion.

When she spotted me, she pulled her window open. "How'd it go?" she whispered loudly.

"Not good. I think Thomas offed Jill." My voice broke as I said it.

Piper shook her head in denial, teeth caught over her lower lip. "What are you going to do?"

It was an excellent question. I shrugged at her and said, "I made a date with the devil."

"What are you talking about?"

"Winthrop. I made a date with him tomorrow night and plan to capture him. If I turn in my Creator, I may have a shot."

"Are you crazy?" she hissed. "He's a crazed killer!"

"Sadly, my options are limited," I retorted dryly, kicking at the dewy grass with my sneaker.

"I'll be right down. I can help you plan," she volunteered, starting to pull her window closed.

"Stop!" I forgot to whisper and she shooshed me. "You can't get involved. It's way too dangerous for you. I'll figure it out on my own."

"I can handle it." She started to close her window again.

"I said no, Piper." My voice was like steel.

"Don't tell me what to do! You can't boss me around like I'm some sort of little kid. You need all the help you can get right now. I might be your only hope."

"Heaven help me if that's the case," I said sarcastically. "I can't capture Winthrop and worry about protecting you as well."

"Fine!" Piper slammed the window down, flipped me off and threw her curtains closed. Great. Things were just great.

Twelve

I sat on the couch feeling like I didn't have a friend in the world. Oh yeah, I didn't. How silly of me to forget. I was about to figure out my next step when the scent of vanilla wafers caught my attention.

"Hey, Aunt Chloe," I said softly over my shoulder.

"Those new ears of yours are something else, missy," Aunt Chloe said as she padded into the family room wearing fleece slippers and an oversized robe. I gave her a halfhearted smile when I noticed she was carrying a heaping bowl of ice cream, but didn't bother to correct her. I couldn't hear much better but I could smell everything.

She took a post opposite me in one of the large over-stuffed chairs and nearly disappeared. She swore under her breath and struggled to sit upright. "I love your mother dearly, but I hate her taste in furniture. A body should be able to sit in a chair and stay put, not sink into a pool of fluff."

I jumped up to help her. When she was finally seated properly, she took a bite of ice cream and said, "You look like you lost your best friend."

I snorted at her but smiled in spite of myself. Aunt Chloe had a gift for understatement.

"Piper is pissed at me and Thomas, well, Thomas . . ." I trailed off, not wanting to tell her the truth: that he wanted to kill me.

She nodded in sympathy. We sat in companionable silence a while longer, she eating her ice cream and me—well, I was drowning in my own misery, wishing I could eat her ice cream as well.

"Did I ever tell you about the love of my life?" she said suddenly.

I raised my eyebrows in surprise. Aunt Chloe never married but I always thought she preferred to be independent.

She regarded my look and chuckled. "Yes, I know what you young people think. Someone my age who never married probably hates men. You thought I buttered my toast on the other side, didn't you?"

I tried to object, but instead my mouth just sort of hung open and wobbled about like a big fish gasping for its last breath.

"No. No. Don't deny it. The way I saw it was, if I couldn't marry the love of my life I wouldn't marry at all. Wouldn't be fair to the fellow who came after him."

Wow, Aunt Chloe had a love of her life. Who'd have thought?

"What happened?" I asked, not sure if fate or tragedy had kept them apart.

"It was during the war. I wasn't much older than you when we met. God, he was magnificent."

"How could you have been so young?" I asked skeptically. After all, Aunt Chloe was known to exaggerate on occasion.

"Times were different then. I went to nursing school when I was sixteen. Not much for young women to do back then, career-wise. I graduated when I was barely eighteen and was called upon to serve my country right after. I was pretty wet behind the ears and with the war, well, I grew up real fast."

"Did you know him long?" I was fascinated that she could have been a surgical nurse at such a young age.

"No, not long. But it didn't matter. Our eyes met and we both knew it. You don't meet your soul mate and not recognize him." She wagged her spoon at me to emphasize her point.

"So what happened?" I asked eagerly.

She sighed deeply, put her spoon and empty bowl down on the side table and astounded me with her answer. "I killed him."

"Come again?"

She nodded in affirmation. "Yes, I had to. It was the only humane thing to do."

"Aunt Chloe, what in the world happened?"

"I told you we met in the war. I met him in France before he was being shipped to Germany. We spent two wonderful days together before he left. Then we planned to see each other again. He came to see me three more times before they brought him in on a stretcher. He was deathly pale and we couldn't get a strong pulse. I was heartbroken when he stopped breathing. Well, that was it.

"They toe-tagged him and it was on to the next wounded soldier. But I wouldn't leave him. I was convinced it was all a big mistake. He couldn't be dead, not my Ned. No one could tell me different. I don't know how much time passed. I sat next to him, holding his hand while his sweet face was covered. I want to say he must have squeezed my hand, but I can't be sure. Anyway, I looked under the sheet and he was staring up at the ceiling, as calm as you please.

"I was so relieved, I was crying and laughing and throwing myself over him. I made quite a scene, I must say."

I smiled at her, imagining the joy she must have felt.

"I jumped up to tell the captain who was in charge that Ned was alive. I got maybe ten feet away and heard the most awful scream. I turned back and Ned was standing over a wounded soldier and he was biting his neck. My sweet Ned was drinking this man's blood and that boy was a-screamin' something awful. I ran back toward them, convinced I could pull Ned off but I couldn't. He was too strong, too thirsty to hear me plead. I could tell then and there that the creature before me wasn't my Ned anymore. He was something else entirely.

"There were rows of wounded boys around. I had to protect them, they were in my care. I couldn't let Ned have his way with them. So I broke a chair and took one of the legs and when Ned moved to his next victim, I staked him through the heart."

I sat stunned at her revelation. I had no idea. None. She'd never said a word to me.

"So now you know."

"I-I don't know what to say. Did he die right away?" It was cruel for me to ask but I wanted to know. I *had* to know.

She sighed deeply. "I'm not a large woman and Ned was a strapping man. I didn't have the strength it took to force the wood in all the way. Our eyes locked; I thought I was a goner. Instead, he grabbed the stake and together—well, together we managed the feat. He helped me, my poor sweet Ned. He knew what had to be done and he helped me."

I stared at her, unable to think of anything that would be the slightest bit appropriate in response to her story. So I said lamely, "I am so sorry, Aunt Chloe. I don't know what to say. You must hate me."

She looked at me in surprise. "What in the world makes you think that? I didn't tell you that story to hurt you, girl. I told you to help you."

"I don't understand. I must remind you of what happened to Ned. You of all people understand what it must be like to be me. I can't believe you aren't grinding a stack of stakes right now."

She stood up and rushed to my side. Her frail arms encircled me. "Now what makes you say a crazy thing like that? You aren't anything like Ned, Colby. He was a full vampire and freshly risen. They have an awful thirst then. When you were freshly risen, how many times did you feed? Once? Twice? You are different, special. You aren't like the others. You are still the Colby I know and love. That hasn't changed, you haven't changed." She smiled at me and pointed to my heart. "At least where it matters, you haven't changed."

I hugged her tightly. She was an amazing woman, my Aunt Chloe, and I never knew it. "I should have visited you more. I'm sorry."

She waved her hand at me in dismissal. "None of that. It's the here and now that matters."

I nodded in agreement. I couldn't worry about the past; it was the future I needed to protect. "Thanks, Aunt Chloe. I have some studying I have to do."

I stood up and grabbed all the paperwork I'd copied at the vampire library. An idea was starting to form in my head.

"Are you studying for your scholarship interview tomorrow?" she ventured. I gave myself a mental slap. I'd completely forgotten all about the interview, but now it didn't matter. The future wasn't just about me anymore.

"No, I have something more important to do." I ignored the surprised look on her face and went upstairs with my research.

Thirteen

I stayed up all night working on my Tribunal presentation. Capturing Chuck wasn't my problem. The *system* was my problem. And the system needed to change.

I skipped school and continued my research. I finally fell asleep out of sheer exhaustion and awoke close to sunset. I had just enough time to shower and meet the university board member for my scholarship interview.

I arrived with barely a moment to spare. Pam and Tim were already seated and fielding questions from a nondescript man in his late forties wearing an overcoat over chinos and a blazer, as well as leather gloves. The room temperature seemed fine to me, but I barely had a pulse. I noticed Pam clutching her sweater close together so perhaps it was a bit chilly in the room. Or maybe she was nervous. Hard to tell with her.

"I apologize for being late," I murmured to Mrs. Gillman, who nodded in understanding. She introduced me to the PSU interviewer, Mr. Holloway, and I apologized to him as well.

"No worries, Ms. Blanchard, we were just getting started. I heard about your earlier, ah, ordeal and just wanted to let you know I am very impressed with your making an appearance here today, under the circumstances."

I nodded to him and glanced at my competitors. Pam fumed silently but Tim seemed oblivious to everything, except Mr. Holloway. The intense scrutiny didn't seem to bother either of them so I ignored it and sat down in the empty chair.

Mr. Holloway scribbled something on the top of a packet of information about the college, then gave it to me. A handwritten note, thanking me for coming in. Maybe I could milk the sympathy thing? Once I sat down, Mr. Holloway directed his next question to me.

"Colby, please tell me your take on Darwin's theory of evolution."

"Only the strong survive?"

"Yes."

"I guess I would need you to clarify your position on 'strong,' Mr. Holloway."

"What do you mean?"

"Well, strength is perception. If you were to ask anyone who was stronger, a cockroach or a human being, I think most people would say a human being. After all, a person can easily squish a cockroach. But, after a nuclear explosion, the cockroach will be the only living creature to survive. So who is stronger in that context?"

"So you disagree with Darwin?" Mr. Holloway pressed.

"If your interpretation of strong is an ability to adapt and evolve, then I would say, yes, the strong will survive. But the strongest is not always the brightest and therefore they jeopardize their own existence."

My fellow students were staring at me with something akin to awe and pity. It wasn't a good sign. I was so tired and making little sense.

"Explain, please."

"Let's take the crown heads of Europe in the earlier centuries. They owned everything, had more than the peasants could ever hope for and believed they were superior. They believed it so much they thought the only way to keep the royal blood pure was to only marry others with royal blood.

"When you narrow the gene pool that much, you just exacerbate the genetic abnormalities, increasing the chance of abnormal propagation. In other words, you get a lot of screwed-up royalty, from genetic disorders like hemophilia to outright insanity. So were they stronger? Eventually you interbreed your royal line into nothingness because none of the offspring can survive. Look at dogs."

Okay, so now I was just letting the lack of sleep, the injustice of my situation and my dislike for those tiny toy poodles take over my interview.

"Excuse me?" Mr. Holloway said.

"You know, purebred dogs," I clarified. "They are so

interbred that many have serious problems, but they cost a lot more money than a mutt. Why? Because they have papers. However, the owners will spend tons of money treating these problems even though many purebreds will die sooner than a regular dog. In the end, the pureblood dogs will die out and the only option left will be the strong, adaptive mongrel that is the loyal, lovable anchor of the American family today."

I smiled sweetly to take the bite out of my rampage. Mrs. Gillman chose this moment to interrupt the interview process by calling a recess. She took me aside and asked how I was feeling.

"Oh, I'm fine, Mrs. Gillman. Never better," I assured her a little too brightly. I was scheduled to capture or kill my vampire Creator in a couple of hours and then defend my existence, but other than that, I was superpeachy.

"Well dear, that's good to hear. I think we have enough information from you at this time. You are free to go."

"I'd really like to finish my interview," I argued.

She gave me a pitying look. "Dear, you are finished. Er, that is to say, you're finished with your portion of the interview today. Thanks for coming in."

It was safe to assume after this completely whack interview that I could safely cross off PSU as a collegiate option. Good-bye scholarship, hello community college.

As I made my way out of the room, I couldn't help but notice how Pam beamed with happiness and Tim avoided eye contact like the plague. I slunk out the side door as quickly and silently as possible.

Even though I wanted to go home and crawl into bed to hide in shame, my stomach wasn't going to let me off that easy. I was hungry. It was time to feed. I drove to the Krispy Kreme and parked my car in their well-lit parking lot. If I was lucky I could find a quick meal. If I was really lucky, I could also capture Chuck.

After checking out the area carefully, I walked across the street to the dimly lit parking lot of a home improvement store and sat down on the concrete pavers display by its front entrance.

Everyone cruised this street; people stopped to chat, hang out and deal in the parking lot. I watched some likely candidates park their low-riding truck with bass-blaring stereo system pretty close to me. Two guys popped out wearing baggy pants and knitted skull caps. I snorted at the Posers. Nothing was funnier than rich white kids pretending to be from the ghetto.

All I needed to hear was the ever-so-famous line, "Yo, what up, dawg?" answered with "Just keepin' it real, yo," to make my evening complete.

I didn't recognize them; they probably went to Newport or one of the other schools. They stood leaning against their shiny red ride, bobbing their heads to the beat and stealing glances at me.

Finally, after a couple of minutes, the taller of the two said something in my direction.

"Whatcha doing all alone out here? Waiting for a ride? We could give ya one." His buddy laughed in appreciation of the innuendo and they tapped fists.

I stood and walked their way, my internal organs shaking with the beat of their bass. "Actually, I'm more in the mood for a bite to eat."

This caused a few guffaws from my prey, as they whispered stupid crude jokes about having something for me to eat all right. How come guys one-on-one were usually so sweet but put them in packs and they were reduced to the lowest common denominator?

I casually took out my head gear and popped it on. They were shocked into silence—and then started laughing! Oh yeah, did I strike fear into the hearts of men or what? I assured myself they were truly terrified of my steel fangs beneath all their mirth-filled bravado.

I took off my sunglasses and looked one in the eyes then the other and both quieted down quickly. They stood transfixed as I stepped in front of them.

"Gentlemen, could you pleash turn down the mushic a bit?" I was proud of how quickly I was mastering my fang-induced speech impediment.

The guy closest to the window reached in and turned it down a decibel or two.

"Ah, lovely. Thank you. Don't move. This won't hurt at all." They stood completely still as I advanced toward one neck and then the next. I took no more than a cup or so total and made sure I licked the puncture wounds. As a thank-you, I left a small hickey for each of them. In a few short moments I was done, and took off my headgear before I spoke again.

"Now, the story is you found two really hot chicks in the parking lot who made out with you—the proof is in the hickeys. Too bad you lost their digits."

I was going to leave when I decided the community needed my services on this one. "Oh yeah, and you no longer like to play your stereo so loud you bounce in the seats. Also, the unwashed hair look is out."

They nodded in unison and I calmly walked away. I was almost out of the parking lot when I heard them get back into their truck and drive away. They did not turn their music back up and I smiled at my good deed for the day.

"Now don't you look proud of yourself?"

I wasn't paying any attention to my surroundings so Chuck managed to sneak up on me. I guess no good deed goes unpunished after all.

Fourteen

"I thought we were meeting later tonight?" I asked, looking around for some sort of weapon or kidnapping tool that would enable me to truss him up and take him to court with me. I was completely unprepared to take action in that moment.

"Tell me, Colby, don't you like to feed? Where is your passion for the hunt? The thrill of the chase? The delicious satisfaction of taking lifeblood from another?" he questioned.

My stomach rolled at the picture he painted. "Dude, it's just lunch. Chill."

"You must think you are better than the rest of them, don't you? You don't fight the same ancient cravings, the wanton lust for destruction and darkness. Oh, how we could conquer the world together."

"You're beginning to sound like a broken record, Chuck."

Not that I'd ever seen a real record, but my father always said this to me when I harped on wanting the same thing over and over again.

"Come away with me," he commanded in a whisper, looking deep into my eyes using all his vampire powers of persuasion to bend me to his will.

I was surprised that part of me wanted to please him, make him happy.

"I'm just not sure," I hedged, trying to fight off the compulsion.

"It is time for us to settle this, Colby."

I suddenly realized that he was right. It was now or never but not the way he meant it. Chuck was right in the sense that we were the same. We were victims. He hadn't asked for what happened to him any more than I'd asked for it. This life of loneliness had driven him crazy and at that moment I realized I couldn't lead him like a lamb to the slaughter.

Despite what he'd done to me, I felt sorry for him. Taking him back to the Tribunal would be like signing his death warrant. At one time that would have thrilled me but after all the research I'd done about vampires, half-bloods and the history of our people, I couldn't really blame him for wanting to have a family and not be alone anymore.

But my newfound understanding didn't mean I was going to hang with him either.

"Good-bye, Chuck. And good luck," I said to him. Then I surprised him by turning away from his intense gaze with little effort and opening my car door. By the time I turned over the engine, he was nowhere in sight and I couldn't help wonder if I hadn't just made the biggest mistake of my life by letting him go, or by not going with him.

It was too late. I'd made my decision. It had stopped being all about me when Jill Schneider was killed. I was fighting for all of us now. Even Chuck. How was that for irony?

I went home and reviewed my defense again. Like it or not, it was all I had now. Satisfied that I was as prepared as I was going to get, I went to bed. I dreamed of Thomas and woke up depressed.

I spent the rest of the evening with my family, basking in the glow of their acceptance and love. None of us was saying aloud what we were really thinking, that this evening was perhaps our last one together.

I thought about calling Piper, but decided it wasn't the best idea under the circumstances. I didn't want her doing something crazy in a last-ditch effort to help me.

Thomas and Carl escorted me to the hearing. Actually, they picked me up and drove me there to assure I wouldn't get lost on my way to the Tribunal offices, which were located in downtown Seattle. It was a very nice space, requiring a card key to access the floor from inside the elevator. I was impressed with the view from the lobby area and pointed it out to Carl, who just looked at me like I was crazy. As did the receptionist. Obviously, I was in a bit of denial for the reason I was there in the first place.

We waited quietly. The evening sky was full of stars, not a cloud was in sight. Thomas turned to speak to me. "Colby, I want you to know that I will do everything I can to assure the successful outcome of your trial."

I smirked at him. "Define successful."

For all I knew he could very well be telling me that he thought relieving me of my Undead status was successful. I tried not to think of his betrayal. It tied my stomach in knots and made my heart hurt.

He didn't try to speak to me again, for which I should have been grateful, but I was not. What I really needed was a hand to hold and there wasn't a friendly face in the house. The receptionist told us we could go in and I wondered if she had any idea who she worked for or if she was a vampire herself. She wore a gray skirt and jacket with sensible heels.

Probably an old-school bloodsucker, I thought somberly.

She led us through a large set of double doors made of rich walnut, which were very imposing and reminded me of a judge's chambers in television shows. The Tribunal was seated on the far side of the room behind a huge, ornate conference table. A stenotype machine was located to the rear of the room, close to the doors, and the receptionist took her place there. I sat facing the Tribunal, my back to her, in the single plain chair provided for me. I thought Thomas might have squeezed my shoulder in support when I sat down but I couldn't be sure. He and Carl took their seats to the left of me against the wall.

There were three head vampires and I looked each over carefully. The first Prince was actually Mr. Holloway, the PSU representative who'd interviewed me for a scholarship earlier. Was I screwed or what? The second gentleman appeared to be in his mid-forties, balding, with his mouth held in a cruel slant. No lips. The man next to him was much younger, around thirty, with thick blond hair and laughing blue eyes. *I might have a shot persuading that one,* I thought.

Behind them sat five other people, two of which were female. I couldn't help thinking how ridiculous it all looked. *These are ancient vampires who survived thousands of years of blood wars and revolutions. We should be meeting in some huge castle, not in some stuffy conference room overlooking the Puget Sound.*

I stifled a giggle. *Oh no, not now.* When faced with overwhelming situations, I tended to get the giggles. That isn't to say I don't take these situations seriously, but to relieve pressure or uncomfortable situations, I tend to laugh. I tried to hide the laugh by coughing and was offered some water, which I gratefully took.

"Colby Blanchard, do you know why you have been summoned to come before the Tribunal?" the receptionist asked.

I turned to answer her. "Yes, I believe so," I said, proud my voice didn't break.

"Kindly direct your answers to the elders in front of you."

I frowned at her and looked back at the Tribunal leaders. Were they really going to deliver every question through the

receptionist seated behind me and expect me to answer looking forward?

"Miss Blanchard, how do you plead to the crime of being
Undead without a license?" she continued.

I thought about that for a moment. Thomas had told me
to say not guilty and then plead my case. It had sounded like
the most logical course of action until I had found out he requested to be my executioner. For all I knew, he was sharpen-
ing his stake as I spoke. I thought of poor Jill Schneider and
knew it was now or never. It was either all about me or all
about my people. I took a deep breath and said, "Guilty as
charged."

There were gasps among the peanut gallery behind the
Tribunal and the blond Prince actually dropped his pen in
surprise. I stole a glance at Thomas, who looked forward
without a hint of expression. Carl, on the other hand, seemed
to take on a greenish hue. *I hope he doesn't hurl,* I thought
with a pitying look at the plush cream carpet.

"Excuse me?" the receptionist said uncertainly.

"I said guilty as charged." I didn't hear the rat-a-tat of her
typing machine so I turned around and said, "Go ahead and
type that. We can wait." She looked from me to the Tribunal,
fingers poised in the air, unsure what to do next.

I was surprised when Mr. Holloway spoke up. "Miss Blanchard, you realize by admitting your guilt that we have no
choice but to relieve you of your Undead status, don't you?"

I took a moment to look him over. He wasn't wearing his

trench coat for this interview but he still had on his gloves. The guy was just odd.

He continued, "Would you like to change your answer?"

I fidgeted a bit with my belt charm before taking another deep breath. "I will not change my answer, sir. I do not recognize the power of this court to uphold or carry out any ruling against me. Therefore I have nothing to fear. You are not a court of my peers."

This caused a scandalized buzz of whispers that demanded gavel action.

"You dare suggest the Tribunal is not in control here?" Mr. Holloway demanded.

"No sir. You have the gavel, the big table and the cool chairs. You're in charge. I just don't see how I apply to your rules."

The blond vampire looked intrigued. "Explain," he said.

"My summons was very specific when calling me to vampire court. Since receiving it, I have been told repeatedly by the Tribunal Investigators that I am not a vampire but a half-blood, a condition neither acknowledged nor recognized by the vampire community. So, based on these facts, it is clear that this court *does not* have jurisdiction over my Undead status."

If they wanted to play by the rules, then they needed to fix the rules. They didn't want half-bloods in their community? Well then they needed to find a place for us. No more getting all medieval on our ass.

"Intriguing argument, Miss Blanchard. What makes you think your actions are above the Tribunal?"

"You misunderstand my statement, Mr. Holloway. I don't believe I'm above the Tribunal, only that the Tribunal does not acknowledge my people, and therefore cannot possibly have dominion over us."

"Miss Blanchard, you are a solitary figure in court today. You have no people."

"Exactly, so this brings me to my next point. I am here to lodge a countersuit against the Tribunal. It seems your Investigators are criminally liable for attacking my people without filing for a Blood War. According to your own rules, 'No Undead shall attempt retribution without first filing a Blood War Sanction.' I have paperwork citing at least eight known instances of such actions."

I pulled out my notes from the black Marvin the Martian briefcase at my feet. It was either this or my backpack and I thought the black briefcase was better than the backpack with key chains. At least I'd worn a stylish pantsuit for the occasion.

"This is outrageous!" the older Prince declared, his eyes bulging from his jowly head. I was concerned he would give himself a stroke but no one else seemed to come to his aid so I schooled my features to reflect polite interest.

"Sir, the vampire community has been sadly lacking in responsibility for its actions for quite some time now. I am merely the messenger calling these unscrupulous actions into question. Your community cannot control its rogues, who in turn create another race, which in turn is exterminated for being the byproduct of your ineptness."

It could hardly be considered the best course of action to practically accuse the Tribunal of genocide, but my hope was to put them on the defensive. It wasn't fair that they'd created this situation and it wasn't fair that innocent people suffered for it either.

"Miss Blanchard, you expect this Tribunal to entertain your frivolous lawsuit and put aside the more serious matter of your unlicensed status?" said the oldest Prince.

"Not at all, sir. I expect this Tribunal to follow the laws they put forth over two hundred years ago to govern the vampire community. As soon as my people are acknowledged as part of that community, I will accept any ruling you dictate over my unlicensed status. But unless and until I am acknowledged I can't and won't be held to the same rules and standards as other vampires. It's quite a pickle, isn't it?" I concluded smugly.

The gavel was back in play, attempting to quiet the vampires in the room. I took close note of the expressions and attitudes of all bystanders to try and guess what they were thinking. The concensus seemed unanimous: they didn't like me but I did have a point.

Mr. Holloway stood up and said, "Miss Blanchard, your conduct and countersuit is a matter that requires deliberation. Therefore, I shall call a recess and adjourn these proceedings until tomorrow evening when we will reconvene at midnight."

"Thank you, sir," I replied, gathering up my paperwork to turn in to the stenographer. If they thought I was kidding, they were in for a shock. My countersuit was even notarized, though I was sure the woman at the bank was skeptical of my story about a mock trial for a high school law class.

I knew it was only a temporary reprieve, but I couldn't help feeling a little proud of myself. In the end I might get exterminated but half-bloods would be recognized within the vampire community and have laws protecting them. Hmmm, when I thought of it that way, I wasn't beaming with pride. Sure, it was a noble deed and all, but I would still be dead.

Carl and Thomas escorted me out of the building and into their car.

"You guys don't need to follow me around. I'm not going to run away or anything."

"We are not escorting you to keep you from fleeing. We are protecting you in case any vampire who disagrees with your politics decides to take matters into their own hands," Carl said.

That certainly took the spring out of my step.

Fifteen

"What happened to the plan? You know—the one where you didn't cause a half-blood revolution and infuriate an ancient race of sinister Undead?" Thomas asked.

"It made sense at the time." I glanced over my shoulder to see if we were being followed. He practically flung me into the backseat of the car and then joined me. Carl drove.

"Colby, I can't even begin to tell you what you have done. Have you any idea the repercussions of your actions in the hearing today?" Thomas was working himself into a fine fit.

"Look, Thomas, if I had done things your way I might have been granted a license. I stress the word 'might.' And then what? Live as an outcast in the vampire community for an eternity? Doesn't sound like an appealing way to spend the rest of time. By forcing them to acknowledge my predicament,

I'm giving other half-bloods a chance, which they don't currently have. Sure, it means less business for you, but I'm confident you can find something else to do with your time."

Thomas was sputtering by the time I was finished. "You silly, vapid, frivolous child!! Is that all you think you are to me? A job to be carried out and then off to the next? Bah!" He grabbed my shoulders to shake me and then just as suddenly released them. I dropped back into the seat with my mouth hanging open. I was trying to tick him off but not to the degree that he completely lost his cool.

What was I supposed to think? He'd asked to be my executioner! That hardly reassured me that he wanted me to win. We traveled the rest of the way home in silence, with Carl driving and Thomas and I sitting as far away from each other as possible.

Both my parents and Great-Aunt Chloe rushed out the front door to greet us. I was practically pulled from the car by my father, who hugged me fiercely, as did my mother and aunt, my briefcase crushed between us.

"We will return for you tomorrow at eleven P.M.," Thomas announced, and they sped away.

"What is Thomas talking about?" my mother asked, tears flowing freely from her eyes.

"I'm not done in court yet. They called a recess until tomorrow."

"What does that mean?" Dad demanded.

"I don't know, Dad. Can't be too bad, right? If they really wanted to get rid of me then they would have done it already."

I offered this lame insight to make them feel better. I hated what this hearing was doing to my family. When I left earlier they didn't know if it would be the last time they would ever see me. Now it was stretched out to another day.

"I'm gonna go talk to Piper," I told them.

"It's awfully late, dear," my mother reminded me. I looked up at her bedroom window and saw the light still on.

"She's still up," I assured Mom as I hurried across our driveway into her side yard. I waited until my family went back inside before picking up a small stone to throw at the window. It hit the shutter with some force so I tossed the next one gently. That one didn't even make it to the second floor.

Muttering to myself, I looked down for some more stones when the scent of a bakery outlet caught my attention.

"What are you doing here?" I demanded to the seemingly empty yard.

Chuck sauntered toward me from behind the twenty-two-foot speedboat Piper's dad kept on the side lawn.

"Is that any way to greet your only family?"

"Where are my manners? What *in the hell* are you doing here?"

He kept coming closer until we stood a couple feet apart. I was thankful Piper hadn't heard the pebbles. The last thing I needed was to worry about her safety with Chuck around.

"So, you're still here." He made this observation somewhat dryly.

"Not much gets past you," I retorted snottily.

"Colby, Colby, Colby. It has come to this now? You are

demanding that vampire society acknowledge the half-bloods? Why would you do that? It can't happen, you know."

To say I was surprised that he knew what I did at the hearing would be a shock to say the least. There hadn't been many people there and I knew Carl and Thomas wouldn't squeal. Did Chuck have someone on the inside? Was that how he evaded capture?

"You shouldn't believe everything you read in the '*Undead Enquirer*'."

He threw his head back and laughed. "Ah, Colby. That's what I love about you. Our eternity together will never be dull."

I shook my head at him. "There won't be an eternity together, Chuck. I'm not going with you. I'm taking my chances with the Tribunal."

His lips straightened into a cold, hard line. "Why are you fighting me on this? I offer you salvation but you'd rather run into the arms of certain death. Why? *Why?*"

I jumped at his hard voice and how quickly he could change demeanor. Something was just not right about ol' Chuck; being ostracized could do that to a vampire.

"Because I can change things. I can make them better for all Undead like me."

"They will never grant you vampire status. You will be executed and forgotten."

He sounded so sure of himself, so cocky.

"What makes you so smart? You're just a lowly rogue on the run. You're living on borrowed time as it is."

"I'm no lowly rogue! I am free to do what I want, when I want. They can't catch me, ever."

"What makes *you* so sure? I don't want to live my life one step ahead of the Investigators!" I still had no intention of going anywhere with him, but I needed to know how he'd found out what had transpired at my hearing.

"Is that what keeps you from coming with me? Fear? My dear, sweet Colby, we can do what no one else can do." He seemed to relax when he thought he was getting past my reservations.

"What's that? Dodge stakes?"

"I will protect you, Colby."

"How? Do you have powerful friends who will keep us safe? No one is going to risk his neck for a rogue," I scoffed, scorning his assurance. *Please, please get mad enough to get careless.*

"Family looks out for each other, Colby. It's like I told you the first time we met." He reached a hand out to mine, his other hand in the shadows. My vampire senses were practically screaming in alarm.

I put my hand out, as though to clasp his and said, "The first time we met, you threw me in a ditch." And I yanked him forward, kneeing him in the groin . . . again. I caught him off guard, to say the least. I took my briefcase and swung it at his face with all my might. It made contact but, due to its nylon exterior, did little damage.

He growled, still unable to stand upright, and lunged for

me. His hand came out of the shadows holding a wicked-looking knife. A knife made entirely of wood. So much for family.

I dodged the stake, but it was very difficult: my heels kept sinking into the grass and moving like a cat was impossible. I kicked my shoes at his head, making contact once. He swore at me.

I ran around to the other side of the boat, looking for a weapon of any kind. The perfectly manicured lawn offered me little hope of finding stray building material. Damn the suburbs!

"Why are you doing this?" I demanded, looking under the boat for his feet so I could keep track of him. "What about all that talk of family?"

As we circled the boat I suddenly lost sight of Chuck's shoes. Wildly, I looked around for him—then he dropped on me from above. He'd leapt over the boat! Stupid vampire superpowers!

I struggled to get back up but he planted a foot on my chest and I heard the crack of ribs breaking. I was sure it would have felt much worse if I were mortal, but it sure knocked the wind out of me.

All of a sudden, I knew the truth.

"You killed Jill." I gasped as he applied more pressure. "They were going to grant her a license and you killed her!"

"Stupid council. She cried so pitifully on the stand, telling how her parents had disowned her for being Undead and she had nowhere else to go. Made me sick to hear how she pleaded and begged for her life, swearing her loyalty to the Tribunal Princes when she refused to come with me, her Creator. I ask you, why? Why not come with me?" He was asking me this question while holding me down with a boot and waving a stake in his hand.

"Maybe it's your people skills?" I offered and he stomped down harder. Despite myself, I cried out in pain.

"All I wanted was to have my family whole again." He looked so sad staring down at me that I almost felt sorry for him. I stress the word "almost" because he was going down now that I knew it was him and not Thomas who did in poor Jill Schneider.

Suddenly, the sound of gravel raining against the back fence caught Chuck off guard, and I used that moment to grip his foot and push up with all my might. I surprised him just enough that he stumbled backward, tripping over something lying on the ground, and fell hard.

I watched in horror as he went down and sort of stopped in midair, arms waving about wildly, staring at some strange object protruding from his chest. Winthrop had impaled himself on the white picket fence that divided my and Piper's lawns. I rolled to my knees and saw Piper, in a black trench coat over her pajamas, still crouched on the grass where Chuck had tripped over her. Her eyes were closed tightly and she was in the fetal position.

"Piper." I grunted, clutching my chest. "Are you okay?"

"Is he dead?" she asked, still clenching her eyes shut.

Chuck was still thrashing around on the fence, unknowingly driving the post deeper into his body with his futile attempts to escape.

I pulled myself all the way up and moved closer to him. His eyes seemed wild and unfocused. I couldn't bear to see all his flapping around like a fish on the shore, so I told Piper to help me get him off the post.

Piper shook her head and refused to get up so I attempted to remove Chuck myself. I tried grabbing his arm and shoulder to try to lift him off when he pulled me closer.

"Colby." He gasped. "Take my ring, take it to the council."

Piper approached us cautiously still shaking her head. She must have felt she'd done her part saving me and wasn't about to let the crazy vampire off his pike, but she did manage to stand next to us. She shrieked when blood flooded out of Chuck's mouth. I pulled the ring off his hand and tugged Piper away from him.

He sort of melted from the inside out until there was nothing left but dust. Dust and the clothes he'd worn.

Despite Piper's protests, I looked through his pants for clues and found a set of keys, a wallet and a note written on Tribunal stationary that said, "Son, she must be eliminated tonight."

I stared hard at the elegant, spidery handwriting for a long time. I recognized it.

"What did you find?" Piper whispered from a safe distance. Nothing was going to convince her to go near our dividing fence again, ever.

"I think I may have found a bargaining chip." If I was right, then maybe I could help half-bloods *and* get a license.

I looked up at Piper who was leaning against the boat, paler than usual, if that was possible. She looked very young without any makeup on. I would remember that expression on her face for an eternity. She was frightened, horrified and a little proud, as though she had accomplished a great feat and was stronger because of it.

I hobbled toward her, still clutching my ribs.

"Let's get you back inside," I said, in a motherly tone.

She bristled instantly and took control, propping me up with her shoulder and arm. "Please, you can't even walk and you're gonna get me home? Do you think any of those broken ribs punctured a lung?"

I tried not to scowl at her question, especially because she sounded so darn hopeful. "Who knows? It's not like I need lungs." She helped me down our driveway to the door and reached out to open it but I stopped her.

"Piper, I-I don't know what I would've done without you. I was wrong to try to stop you from helping me."

"No, you were so right. What was I thinking? I'm no vampire slayer. I saw him jump over the boat from my window and I knew if I didn't do something, you were a goner. So I ran out and threw gravel at the fence."

"That was your great plan? You didn't mean to crouch behind him and help me trip him into the fence?"

"Are you crazy?! I just wanted to make a noise to distract

him. When I realized he might see me I just sort of dropped into a ball to hide."

I laughed, and then groaned in pain. She was no Buffy, but then I was no Angel. Despite that, we made a pretty good team.

*   *   *

After a refreshing bath, only a boot print and a small ache reminded me of what transpired in the yard. My family had already gone to bed and though Piper gallantly tried to stay up with me, around 3 A.M. she couldn't keep her eyes open anymore. We walked to her door together. After she was safely inside, I decided it was time to do a little investigating on my own.

I borrowed my mom's Lexus for the trip downtown. I was going back to the Tribunal headquarters. Mr. Holloway and I needed to have a little chat.

The same receptionist was seated in the lobby. If she looked surprised to see me, she didn't show it.

"I'd like to see Mr. Holloway please."

"I'm afraid that is quite impossible. He is not to be disturbed. You will have your opportunity to meet with him tomorrow, at your designated time." She sneered slightly, confirming my suspicions that she too would prefer if I were whacked.

If there was something I learned about bureaucratic vampires it was that they didn't like scenes. And I, Colby

Blanchard, was all about scenes. So I thanked her politely and walked straight back to where my court appointment had been held. Mr. Holloway's name was on one of the side doors and my bet was that was his office.

"Hey, stop! You can't . . ."

I ignored her as I swept into the conference room. No one in sight. I picked the door to the right and knocked before walking right in.

He sat at a big walnut desk, wearing his signature gloves and blazer. To say he looked shocked to see me would be an understatement. "Hello, Mr. Holloway."

"What are you doing here?" he exclaimed.

"I came here to make a deal." My voice was strong despite the nervousness I was feeling. I mean, how often did a half-blood stand up to a regional vampire Prince and live to tell about it?

"I know about Chuck, er, Winthrop." I bit my lip and looked around his tidy office.

He leaned back and studied me. I opened the note I'd found in Chuck's pocket and held it out in front of me.

"So you expect me to believe you bested him?" His voice was dry with sarcasm.

I guess I should have been happy we weren't going to play the "what are you talking about?" game but still, a little lead time would have been nice so I didn't have to blurt out that Chuck was literally dust in the wind.

I dropped Chuck's license on the desk in front of me. Mr. Holloway's eyes widened in surprise as he picked up the ring, turning it over and over in his gloved hand. Inside the ring were the initials c.w.h.

"You have your ring back, Charles Winthrop Holloway." I waited for his reaction.

He slipped off his right glove and put on the ring. It fit perfectly. "When did you figure it out?" he said calmly.

"I guess it bothered me that you always wore gloves but it was Chuck's obsession with family that tipped me off. I gave him my word when he died and I kept it."

"What word? What did he ask?"

"He asked me to give his license back to the council. Chuck was never a rogue vampire. He was a half-blood, wasn't he? I thought I'd seen him before that night he attacked me. He was a half-blood *you* created without permission," I accused. "You sent him away with your license so he could live freely elsewhere but he came back to you. He came back to family.

"He eluded the Investigators because you would feed him information on how close they were and because he operated mainly during the day, when other vampires couldn't. That's why I recognized him but couldn't place where. He would hang out at my school, in the mall and at games.

"The one thing I just can't figure out is how you got your license off without being dead."

He stared at me for a long time. I wished I had psychic abilities, but Mr. Holloway was just sinister enough that I doubted I would really want to poke around in his brain.

"I loved my son, Miss Blanchard," Mr. Holloway finally said. "Oh yes, he was my biological son. After I was turned,

I could see the lonely, bleak existence without him and I couldn't bear it. I couldn't attain a license but I turned him anyway. In doing so he became *different*. He was not the same man I raised, this Undead version of my son. So I sent him away. When you love someone, it is a simple matter to cut off a finger to remove a ring.

"Thanks to vampire regenerative powers, I simply put it back in place to knit together, but it never healed correctly," he continued. "There was a time it was easy to hide what I had done. Every gentleman wore gloves then. Now, wearing gloves inside is an oddity a young vampire would notice, but the older ones would not. Many of us have a hard time changing our ways to blend in with modern times, we tend to keep to ourselves."

His confession answered my questions but grossed me out as well. He'd cut off his own finger! Eek! Chuck wasn't the only one not right in the head.

"Chuck loved you, Mr. Holloway. He was desperate for family, which is why he kept changing humans to half-bloods. He was just . . . lonely." *And crazy,* I added to myself.

"You think you've won, don't you?"

I snorted at his observation. "Yeah, that's it. Since the day I woke up Undead I've been saying to myself 'I'm such a winner.' "

Mr. Holloway nodded in understanding. I wasn't there to gloat. This was about survival and my right to live.

"The Tribunal is undecided concerning the acknowledgment of half-bloods," he said.

"I'm sure your advocacy of the issue will swing any re-maining resistance."

"And if I don't?"

I dropped a copy of his note to Chuck on his desk next to the license. I knew it was in his hand because he'd given me that sympathy note with my university packet. The writing was a perfect match. If anyone on the Tribunal knew he'd fed Chuck information to elude the Investigators, then Mr. Hol-loway's vampire days were over.

He paused to gather his thoughts and then stood up. I jumped slightly when he rose and was clearly quaking in my boots as he walked around the desk. He noticed my reaction and chuckled without humor. "You are in no harm, Miss Blan-chard. Technically, since you killed Charles, you replace him. You become my daughter."

I shivered at the implication.

"Which means you have my protection, forever. Not a bad thing for someone with your unique background to have, a Prince's protection."

A fat lot of good it did Chuck, I wanted to say but kept my mouth shut.

He stepped toward the filing cabinet to my left and un-locked it. He removed a file that bulged with photos, of all things, and handed it to me.

When he turned to return to his desk, I stopped him with a cautious hand on his shoulder.

"Mr. Holloway, I really am very sorry about Charles." And I was too.

He paused momentarily and nodded. Then, as quickly as the look of shared remorse was there, it was gone and he was back to business, taking his place behind the desk again.

"You will have your license, Miss Blanchard."

"And the half-bloods?" I persisted.

"And the half-bloods will be acknowledged by vampire society."

"Thank you, sir." I was almost out the door when Mr. Holloway spoke again.

"There is an old saying, Miss Blanchard. Be careful what you wish for . . ."

He didn't finish his statement and when we locked eyes, I shivered at the implication. Half-bloods could now exist, but at what price?

Once outside his office, I opened the folder of photos. Some were very old; there were even some painted portraits. Each had two dates listed on the back, rebirth and death. All except one picture—mine. It had the date I was attacked but no death date. I looked at the other pictures again. Some dates were a week apart, some were more. But none was more than a few months.

Whatever the price for our existence, it was worth it.

Sixteen

The doorbell rang insistently. I didn't want to see anyone; I had reserved this evening to wallow in self-pity. A week had passed since I was granted my license and now it was Homecoming night—and I still had no date and no Thomas. He hadn't spoken to me since the final hearing, when all he'd said was congratulations. He must have been pretty disappointed that he wasn't going to be able to "relieve me of my Undead status."

When I reached the door, I could smell cookies. I opened the door quickly, stating bluntly, "Go away," and shut it again in Thomas's surprised face. Thomas looked so handsome in the quick glimpse I'd gotten that I should have slammed the door harder than I did. *Great, now he would know I was weakening and try to worm his way back into my affections.*

"I have a gift for you," Thomas said. My heart constricted. He sounded so good.

I replied, "I don't want a stake through the heart, thank you. Now go away."

I could hear him sigh deeply, though we were separated by a good inch or two of wood.

"Colby, you're going to have to see me sometime. I'm not going anywhere until you open this door."

"Oh well, if you put it that way, I can wait all night. Until the sun comes up. Gee, can you say the same?"

He swore under his breath and then I heard a rhythmic sound. *Thump. Thump. Thump. Thump. Thump.* "You. Are. Driving. Me. Crazy," he said between thumps. He was banging his head against the door and I smiled.

That made two of us. Why did he have to be so cute? Be such a good kisser? Be here in general?

"You're going to crack your head open doing that," I finally told him after a good thirty seconds of head thumping.

"Then. Open. The. Door." *Thump, thump, thump.*

"Oh for heaven's sake," I muttered as I flung open the door. "You're the most stubborn bloodsucker!" I announced, glaring at him.

It took me a moment to realize that Thomas was dressed in a black tuxedo. I blinked at him several times but the image did not fade. Yes, he was standing at my door in formal wear. Seemed a little extreme to dress up just to stake someone and I told him so.

"I am not going to stake you, Colby. I've been telling you

that forever. I have something for you from the Tribunal." He held out a small box.

It wasn't Tiffany's turquoise blue, but a box that size screamed jewelry—and being the weak half-blood mutant vampire that I was, I really wanted to see what was inside.

I accepted the box with a great show of exasperation, as though I was doing him a huge favor by taking it off his hands and really had no interest as to what lay inside, which we both knew was a huge crock of crap, but he allowed me the illusion, at least.

I snapped it open and gasped at the gleaming ring. It was my license. A very modern-looking, delicate crest set in white gold, just for me. I slipped it on my right hand and it fit perfectly. It felt warm and accepting against my skin. I closed my eyes for a moment, squeezing my hand into a fist. I belonged.

Thomas cleared his throat and brought me back to the present. He was holding out a manila envelope.

"What's this?" I asked, taking it from him.

"Open it and see." Thomas was a man of mystery, but his eyes sparkled and a hint of a smile played on his lips. Why was he so darling?! It was unfair and just plain mean!

I ripped open the envelope and pulled the contents out. A letter from the Tribunal was at the top. I read the subject line.

"My job assignment?" I asked uncertainly. I wasn't even seventeen yet and they were giving me a job? "I can't have a job! I've got to study for my SATs and get into college!"

"Look at the next page."

Confused, I flipped past the assignment and found an

acceptance letter from Puget Sound University and then another letter congratulating me on earning a four-year scholarship.

"I-I can't believe it! But I don't understand." I was confused, happy and suspicious all at once. Anything involving Thomas seemed to have that effect on me.

"After you met with the Tribunal, they decided you had a point about the half-blood situation. So, with that in mind, they instituted a new program. The-training-and-acclimation-of-half-bloods-into-vampire-society program."

"Wow! I did that? Amazing. I don't envy the poor sucker who's in charge of that program. No pun intended," I added hastily.

Thomas was grinning ear to ear by now and a deep sense of dread started in the pit of my stomach.

"Oh, no. Say they didn't!"

Thomas thrust out his hand to shake mine. "Welcome to the Tribunal, Colby. I look forward to working with you."

"I can't head up that program. I'm just a kid! Why would they send me to college if they expect me to work for them?"

I was thoroughly confused and not just a little bit pleased. It was a huge responsibility they'd given me. Of course, who else would they assign it to? They kept killing all the other half-bloods so it wasn't as though there were a ton of other vampires with experience being a mutant.

"I suggest you read the rest of the paperwork," Thomas replied with a sweep of his hand, motioning to the couch in the living room where we could both sit down. I began to read my job description.

"How am I going to do all this? *Every* Prince is sending me their female half-bloods? Where are they going to stay? How am I going to take courses and protect them? I can barely protect myself."

"You are special, Colby. You can do this. Besides, it will be easier once you are all living under one roof."

"Say again?" I was certain I hadn't heard Thomas correctly. I planned to live in the dorms the first year and then find a nice, quiet place off-campus.

"The Tribunal has purchased a house for this project. It's at the end of something called Greek Row. Not sure what that is, must be the name of a street close to the college. Anyway, you're all going to live there."

"A house?" I squealed in excitement. "They bought a sorority house and I'm in charge of it?" I jumped up in excitement and did a little victory dance.

Thomas raised an eyebrow at me but I ignored him and kept right on doing the Cabbage Patch, alternating it with a pointed finger in a lame disco imitation.

"I can assume by your expression that this news pleases you?" Thomas asked.

"Duh! Who wouldn't want to head their own sorority?"

"Excellent," Thomas said, standing as well. "Then it is settled. Now go upstairs and change."

I stopped in mid-dance. "Change for what?" I asked, eyeing his formal attire once again.

"For the dance you bemoaned missing. I am here as your escort. Am I not suitably attired?"

"Well, yeah, you look great. But I can't go to the dance now. Piper and I made a deal. We're going to make popcorn and watch old movies tonight, and then make fun of the Homecoming King and Queen when they're announced. Dale is all set to call us when they are crowned at the party."

I pointed to the coffee table filled with Piper's favorite munchies, a stack of DVDs and my neon pink cell phone.

"She'll be here any moment." I was kind of disappointed now that Thomas was here and looking so hot. But I'd made a promise and I wasn't going to screw over Piper because now I had a date and she didn't.

"Yes, that is a dilemma. What if Piper had an escort as well? Then could you both attend?"

"Well, I guess so. If she said it was okay." I wasn't sure where Thomas was going with this conversation. "But it's a moot point because she doesn't have a date and I won't set her up with some loser just so I can go to the dance."

"Your loyalty is admirable. I promise I had no 'loser' in mind." He walked back to the front door and opened it. After a moment, Carl walked in wearing a black tuxedo and I nearly swooned at the sight. Carl and I may have had our differences but yowza! The guy looked like he'd stepped off the cover of *GQ*.

I looked at both men for a moment, then picked up my phone and dialed Piper.

"Hey," she answered. "I'll be over in a second."

"Look out your bedroom window into my driveway."

She paused for a moment and said, "'Kay."

I directed Thomas and Carl to go outside and stand in the driveway facing Piper's house. I turned on the walkway lights to illuminate them both. I stood on the porch and when I could see Piper looking through her window I spoke into the phone.

"What do you think?"

"Is the tall, gorgeous one on the left for me?"

"Yeah."

She took another moment and said, "Tell them to come back in an hour."

Laughing, I replied, "Got it!"

I shooed the guys off for an hour and a half. Piper might only need an hour but this was Homecoming and I wanted to look my best. We could skip eating, since three of us were on a liquid diet. Piper would just have to grab a sandwich while she was getting ready.

*   *   *

She arrived at my house in exactly one hour, dressed in a Spanish flamenco dancer's gown, with a short lace veil attached in her hair, which she wore severely slicked back. Black crystal earrings dangled from her lobes and a matching necklace showed her pale skin to perfection. She even wore a tiny black crystal stud in her nose.

I whistled deep when I saw her. She looked magnificent. "That is quite a dress, my friend. And some serious cleavage."

She curtsied, snapping open a lace fan and gracefully fanning herself, delicately hiding her cleavage from view.

"This corset might just kill me," she admitted and I laughed at her.

"The cost of beauty is never cheap," I offered.

"Way to be dressed," she accused as she sashayed down the hallway toward the kitchen.

"I'm almost done, just let me get the dress on. Be right down. You better eat something before we go," I called out to her as I raced up the stairs.

"On it," came her muffled reply. I heard my mom's cries of admiration and surprise when she saw Piper.

I decided to wear my hair up, with a riot of curls cascading down my back. It was the style I thought would show off the princess tiara most appropriately. My dress for the evening was an icy blue, with spaghetti straps that crisscrossed down my back. The chiffon layers of the skirt floated as I walked, flashing a great deal of leg with each step. To complete the look, I wore strappy silver heels, a silver choker and matching hoop earrings. My license was the only adornment I needed on my hands. I checked myself out in the full-length mirror and nodded in satisfaction. Not too shabby.

I grabbed a tiny silver purse for my phone and lipstick, and then draped a silver wrap over my bare shoulders. Good thing I was Undead or tonight might be a little chilly.

The doorbell rang as I walked down the steps and my mom answered it.

Thomas stepped in and our eyes met. I was happy to see them widen in surprise and admiration. Yes, a girl liked to know when she looked good.

Carl stepped into the house behind him holding a bouquet of red roses for his date. Nice touch.

I could tell the instant he caught sight of Piper. His smile widened, his white teeth flashed and a dimple made an appearance. Who knew Carl was a dimple kind of guy? Usually he was growling at me or threatening me or trying to strangle me.

"*Encantado,*" Carl murmured, bringing Piper's hand to his mouth and kissing it.

I was amused to see Piper blush to the roots of her jet-black hair. She accepted the flowers but my mother quickly confiscated them to put in a vase full of water. Heaven forbid those blooms go another minute without moisture. *Moms.*

She returned with a camera and a single red bud from Piper's bouquet and suggested Piper tuck it into Carl's lapel. Then we withstood a thousand photographs.

Dad wished us all well as we left. A black limousine was waiting for us at the curb. Carl helped Piper into the car and Thomas waved the chauffer aside so he could hold the door open for me himself.

"Now isn't this nicer than whacking me?" I teased him lightly.

He grabbed both my hands and looked deeply into my eyes. "The only reason I requested to be your executioner was to protect you, Colby. Some Investigators hate half-bloods and do unspeakable things to them before they finally end their pain. I could not bear to think of anyone toying with you in such a fashion."

I was surprised by his concern. I could tell he spoke the truth by the intensity of his gaze.

"I would have died in my heart to end your life, but I would have done it to save you further torment."

I gave him a small half smile, full of tenderness and emotion. Then I assured him cockily, "Dude, you sooo could not have killed me."

He laughed and kissed the tip of my nose.

"Hurry up out there. We'll never get to make fun of anyone if you keep gabbing," Piper complained from inside the limo.

I laughed out loud. With Piper around I would never get too uppity, and with Thomas around, I—well, let's just say things would never get boring. Next year I was going to PSU. My job was to run my own sorority house! Imagine the fun we would have. What was the Tribunal thinking?

Super Secret Author Confessions Volume 1

My Worst Date
Ever . . .

In college, I experienced my worst date ever. Feel free to mock my pain . . .

* * *

I had a crush on a boy who worked in the dining hall. After many weeks of flirting, he finally asked me out. He took me to a party at his apartment where, within a half hour of our arrival, he received a phone call from his "other" job. He claimed he was also an on-call janitor for one of the dorms. After apologizing profusely, he changed into spandex shorts (Dude, it was the late '80s), assured me he would return within the hour, and left to fulfill his janitorial duties. I did not see him again until six the next morning.

I was stranded at his apartment with a bunch of people I didn't know. After playing one too many rounds of Quarters, I crashed on his bed. I also sort of . . . threw up on his bed. Anyway, about six in the morning I stumbled downstairs and found him cleaning up. He was so sorry and so sweet. He assured me he kept calling to make sure I was okay because he ended up having to "work" all night. I should have been suspicious, because he was *really* understanding about the whole vomit on his comforter thing. He gallantly offered to drive me back to my dorm after asking me to go to a concert with him the following week.

Once in my own bed, I promptly drifted off to sleep dreaming about our next date. I awoke to a fierce pounding on my door. "Where were you last night?" my friends demanded. I explained about my date and his "other" job. Imagine my surprise to discover my date had left me stranded at his apartment while he went on *another date* with a girl who lived two doors down from me. He took her to a widely advertised dance in the dining hall and entered the spandex competition (he won second place). Then he spent the night with her and returned home in the wee hours of the morning to me, his original date.

The best part of this story? When I confronted this guy, he was most upset that I wasn't going to the concert because he expected me to *reimburse him for the ticket*.

Oh, yes, this is a true story. Sad, but very true.

Eight Things You Didn't Know About Me

1. It took me three days to write 150 pages of *Braced 2 Bite*.

2. I watched every season of *Buffy* in only three weeks. For those of you doing the math, that's approximately six plus episodes a day. Which would explain why I had to write 150 pages of *Braced 2 Bite* in three days.

3. My favorite drink is Mountain Dew and I try to have one of my characters drink it in every book. My secret hope is that someone at Pepsi will offer me free Dew in exchange for the promotion.

4. I currently own twenty-eight pairs of shoes, four pairs of sneakers, six pairs of flip-flops, and five pairs of boots.

5. I am an avid scrapbooker who has all the latest gadgets and paper but doesn't possess a single up-to-date album.

6. Every year, my friends and I have an Oscar party. We dress up in formal wear (complete with tiaras) and pretend we are Joan and Melissa Rivers rating fashions on the red carpet. Then I hit the drive-thru at McDonald's dressed in my finery.

7. When Googling my name (yeah, like you've never done it) I found a company called Robar Guns. They create custom firearms. Now I want to get one just so I can say I'm packing a Robar.

8. I couldn't think of ten interesting things, which is really sort of sad. . . .

My first piece of published work appeared in an elementary-school newsletter when I was in the second grade. Please note the amount of angst I had for fish, which may explain why I never had any pets as a child. . . .

Ode to Fish

Hey, fish you stink
You smell like disinfected odors
When you die, they flush you
Down the toilet and your fish food too.
So don't lose your smell!!
I hate you fish.
You stink. You do! You do! You do!
I am glad I do not like you.
You stay in the water too much.

And now for a special excerpt from
Serena Robar's next exciting novel . . .

FANGS FOR FREAKS

Available from Berkley!

A body launched straight at me from the bushes before I had time to register who or what it was. The force of impact was enough to knock the breath from my lungs, that is, if I breathed. Instead of crushing me with its force, I rolled with his momentum and neatly turned over once, then used my feet to send him flying over my head, crashing into crates of recycling awaiting pick-up on the sidewalk.

Doing a quick flip from my back onto my feet, I, Colby Blanchard, moved toward my would-be assailant without trepidation.

"Are you okay, Cyrus?" I questioned, looking for signs of injury as he lay sprawled among the old newspapers and empty soda cans.

"Mhmph," came his muffled reply as he disentangled

himself from the bins, "finish me?" He stood and I was relieved to find him relatively unharmed.

"What did you say?" I asked again, a bit dubious of his reply. His left pant leg was ripped at the knee and I could see the scraped skin starting to bleed.

The scent of fresh blood filled my senses and I had to take a step back. A familiar ache in the roof of my mouth and the loud rumbling from my stomach reminded me I didn't feed last night. My treacherous hand involuntarily reached for the pocket housing specialized orthodontic headgear embedded with stainless steel fangs. What? Just because I'm fang-handicapped doesn't make me a freak or anything. I can still get the job done ya know. Just not right now. Now it was a battle of wills, between my true self and the inner demon who demanded to feed.

I took a Zen moment and subdued my hunger. It was so not getting the upper hand here. The first rule of thumb was no feeding on friends and I wasn't about to break it because I was feeling a bit peckish.

"I said, why didn't you finish me off? You stood there like some clueless victim waiting for me to find a weapon to take you down."

"Uh, I knew it was you?" It was an obvious answer, but Cyrus was always all business.

For the last eight months, Cyrus had spent two hours a day teaching me how to fight and protect myself. I met him on a routine visit to see my great-aunt Chloe at her condo in Providence Point. Her neighbor, Bits Walker, was bragging about her grandson, a self-defense instructor and former Special Operative in the military. Like anything Bits said, I took it with a grain of salt. After all, she'd been married four times and on last count, she mentioned seven husbands. I wondered if perhaps, she wasn't all there.

But one day, there was Cyrus, holding Bits's yarn as she knitted and listening attentively to her stories. He was smaller than I imagined, with craggy skin and a wicked-looking scar that went across his chin to his left ear, which appeared to be partially missing. He was wiry and muscular. I doubted he had an ounce of fat on his frame.

My thoughts were interrupted by Cyrus digging around the refuse. "What are you looking for?" I asked skeptically. Cyrus was, well, let's just say he and his grandmother were very alike in the sanity department.

"Aha!" he shouted triumphantly, brandishing what appeared to be a sharpened piece of wood.

"You had a stake?!" I gasped incredulously.

"It's like I'm having a conversation with Jell-O," he muttered to himself. "Of course. Did you think I was going to continue attacking you with just my bare hands? You are too far advanced for those tactics. At least I thought you were. I thought you had achieved the black zone."

Oh crap, not the zones again.

When he first started training me, I was in the white zone, which meant I was completely oblivious to my surroundings. Then came the blue zone or was it the green? I could never keep them straight. Anyway, I quickly raced up the zones to the black zone, which meant I was in Ninja-like awareness all the time. Personally, I liked being in the white zone but when you're the most unpopular half-blood Undead in the neighborhood, you can't afford to be in the white zone anymore.

Ever since I was attacked and turned into a vampire—oh excuse me, that would be *half-blood* vampire—I'd become persona non grata in the Undead community. I think I might have been able to live out my days in relative peace and solitude if I hadn't petitioned for half-blood rights and emancipated an entire species. That move made me a little less than popular with the full-blood population. Well, *excuse me* for fighting injustice.

I did such a good job freeing my people, I was elevated to being their Protector, which I am sure was the Tribunal's way of getting rid of all of us. I imagine they were still kicking themselves that not only was I Undead and around, but I was also becoming a pretty kick-ass Protector in the process.

Today was the day I would meet the rest of my half-blood family. Yep, we are going to show those bigoted full-bloods that we're every bit as useful and viable a species and deserve to exist. At least, I hoped so. I hadn't met any other half-bloods yet, but I held high hopes for our success.

"Colby? Hello? Colby Blanchard? Are you even listening to me?" Cyrus asked impatiently.

"Uh, sorry. What were you saying about the zone?"

He sighed in exasperation (he did that a lot with me) and repeated, "Since you refuse to allow me to test your skills in the evening, you have to be in the zone *all the time*."

I held up a hand to stop him. "Yeah, yeah, I get it. I'm sorry. It's just today is the day I meet my new sorority sisters and I'm really nervous."

"Oh, well then, that's fine. I'm sure no one will be out to get you today then."

"Ha-ha," I retorted sarcastically.

"Today of all days you need to be most aware."

It took my aunt Chloe exactly twelve minutes to tell Cyrus what I really was and persuade him to train me. Cyrus had believed her immediately, even though I walked around during the day and didn't have real fangs. I guess it was the incident about his grandmother that did it. I'd insisted on taking Bits to her doctor because she smelled different that day. My super sniffer detected a change in her normal lavender scent. It was a move that saved her life. Bits was on the verge of a heart attack, but thanks to me, she ended up with a bypass and a new lease on life.

He seemed to accept that I was a mutant Undead with limited vampiric powers who needed steel fangs to bite her victims because I had had my canine teeth removed for braces when I was twelve. I mean, it makes perfect sense right? HA! It was my life and even I had a hard time believing it most of the time.

"I wish you would let me teach you defense with weapons," he complained.

We were back to that old argument. I think he knew how close I was to caving on that one.

In the evenings, Thomas, my Vampire Investigator

boyfriend trained with me and we used swords. Actually, it would be fairer to say Thomas used the swords and I just did my best to avoid being beheaded and/or shish-kabobed. Thomas wouldn't train me using a sword yet; he didn't think I was quite ready. Well, his actual words were something along the lines of "you'll poke your eye out" but the gist was the same.

I sighed heavily. "No, just help me avoid the stick."

He gave me his patented you-are-one-crazy-chick look and dropped the subject.

"Are you going to visit Bits today?" I asked.

"Already did. I have to leave tonight for a mission. I won't be back until Monday."

"You're leaving me?" I said in surprise.

"Yeah, I do have paying customers who need my services, you know. Don't worry, Thomas won't leave you alone this weekend, so you should be fine."

"You know, I don't need Thomas's protection to be just fine. I can take care of myself."

"Oh really? Check out your shirt."

I glanced down to see a white chalk mark dead center on my chest. When I looked back at Cyrus, he held the "wooden stake" for me to examine. It was really a large stick of chalk.

"Oh," I said in surprise, realizing that if he was really out to get me, he could have killed me right then.

"You were saying?" His constant superior ways and arrogance were always annoying, but he was particularly obnoxious today.

"Bite me," I replied in my snarkiest tone. Yes, I am the queen of maturity when provoked.

"That's your department," he said dryly and turned to walk away. Looking back over his shoulder he added, "Be safe and don't hesitate to finish the job."

I watched him leave, his body tightly wound, ready to spring if the situation warranted it.

"He's so weird," commented a voice from behind, effectively scaring the daylights out of me.

"*Argh!* Don't *do* that! You could've given me a heart attack!" I squealed, grabbing my chest for dramatic effect.

"The day your heart starts beating . . . I'll be the one having a heart attack."

Piper Prescott was my best friend and occasional arch nemesis. She wore her hair straight to the shoulders, jet-black with burgundy ends. Her nose was pierced, her skin a shade of alabaster rarely found on another living being and she always, always spoke her mind. We were direct opposites in so many ways, but I wouldn't trade our friendship for all the Kate Spade bags in Macy's. Well, usually I felt that way.

"Dude, you are so funny, I forgot to laugh."

We moved to tidy up the recycling that Cyrus scattered and walked into Piper's house to wash our hands.

"So, today's the big day, huh?" Piper asked after folding up the dish towel.

"Yep, tonight I meet the rest of the house. I can't believe it. You're gonna be there, right?" I was nervous about meeting them but proud of my accomplishment at the same time. I'd spent the last year of my life preparing for the moment I would meet the first half-bloods allowed to exist in vampire history. All because of me.

"Oh, I'll be there." Piper smirked. "Wouldn't miss it for the world."

"Do you have to be so negative?" I asked her. Piper was of the opinion that a bunch of girls with nothing in common except being Undead and forced to live together was a recipe for catastrophe.

She opened the fridge and took out a Mountain Dew. "I'm just saying this thing has disaster written all over it."

She tried to open the can but couldn't get her finger under the tab.

"Oh here, give it to me." I used my manicured nail to pop open her soda.

"Are you still biting your nails?" I started to lecture, "Don't you know that everyone looks at your hands and gains an impression about you?"

Piper put her hands over her ears and started to sing, "La la la la, I can't hear you, la la la."

"Oh fine." Piper always resisted my suggestions for self-improvement. I returned her drink and brought the conversation back to my meeting. "And tonight doesn't have disaster written all over it. These girls are lucky to be alive and I bet they are just as excited to meet me as I am to meet them. After all, I *saved* them and, because of me, they get a second chance. You'll see."

We plopped down on a comfy couch in her living room, enjoying the air-conditioning for a moment.

"Where's your mom?"

"She's still at work. We only have a couple of days left until we go to Europe. Even though she is dragging us on a work thing, I'm kind of excited. I miss England," she added wistfully.

Piper spent a summer with her family roaming the European countryside and loved it. She was kind of a Gypsy at heart.

"You'll still be on e-mail right? I know your cell phone won't work over there, but you'll still have Internet access, right?"

"Quit being so nervous. You'll be fine," Piper reassured me.

"Yeah, I know." I started to nibble on the cuticle of my thumb.

"I saw that Thomas was over last night. Is he finally putting out?" Piper asked.

"Piper! What kind of question is that?" I gasped, feigning outrage.

"So that would be a no then."

I debated playing the offended victim but frankly, I needed some advice on this one. "What's wrong with me? We're in constant physical contact. He wrestles with me at training and I'm all, yeah baby come and get it, but he's been a perfect gentleman. It pisses me off."

"I sense a little frustration coming from the Blanchard household," Piper remarked dryly.

I scrunched up my nose, holding my thumb and forefinger up, about an inch apart. "Little bit."

"So why not just ask him what the deal is?"

"It's not that simple. He's old fashioned and obsessed with training me. Like, totally obsessed. It's on his mind constantly. The other day I was in my knit bikini. You know, the purple one? It's totally scandalous!

"Anyway, I'm all prancin' around trying to get his mind off of training and he goes and gives me his sweatshirt to wear, so I won't get cold in the drafty warehouse we work out in. Ohmigod, he doesn't even ask why the hell I am wearing a purple knit bikini to practice or anything, just covers me up and is all business. I must truly disgust him." I finished my tirade with a wail of self-pity.

"Wow."

I punch the sofa cushion next to me.

"Yeah, wow."

"You must look pretty bad in that bikini."

"Piper!!"

She laughed at me. Did I mention Piper can be my arch nemesis *while* she is being my best friend?

"Okay, okay. First of all. Let's think a little, shall we? It's the middle of freakin' August and he gives you a sweatshirt to cover up with so you won't get cold? Hello? It's like, seventy degrees at night. He wanted you covered up because he obviously didn't trust himself to keep it in his pants if he had access to all that naked skin." I hadn't thought of it in those terms before and perked up at the thought of Thomas fearing he would lose control around me.

Piper continued her assessment. "Second, Thomas cares for you a lot. He's been training you hard so you can protect yourself. He doesn't want to lose you. And finally, maybe he's gay?"

I threw the pillow at Piper's head. No guy who kisses a girl like Thomas does could be gay. End of story.

"The last one must be it," I jokingly agreed with her, not completely convinced but feeling much better about things.

After a moment of companionable silence, Piper said, "Colby?"

"Yeah?"

"Quit chewing on your nails."

Brat.